MY SUMMER IN ST. IVES

Don Barr

Between the Lines
PUBLISHING

My Summer in St. Ives is a work of fiction. Unless you have a 12th Century knight show up on your doorstep, all characters, organizations, and events portrayed are either a product of the author's vivid imagination or are used fictitiously.

Original artwork: Don Barr

Republished June 2022
My Summer in St. Ives

Paperback ISBN: 978-1-950502-34-9
eBook ISBN: 978-0-9996556-4-1

Originally published: 2018
Alexander Crowley – A New King in Town

Paperback ISBN: 978-0-9996556-3-4
eBook ISBN: 978-0-9996556-4-1

Between the Lines Publishing
9 North River Road
Suite 248
Auburn ME 04210
www.btwnthelines.com

Printed in the United States of America

MY SUMMER IN ST. IVES

I would like to thank all those people throughout my life who have had no faith in me or offered little inspiration.

Your lack of encouragement has been priceless and without it, this book would not exist.

In contrast those few that have been of influence know who they are, and I could never thank them enough.

St Ives is my favourite place on the planet and hopefully I haven't caused the locals or those that flock there each summer too much offence. The characters you are about to meet and the places you are about to visit are fictitious except where I have used reference for comedic or satirical purposes so anybody identifying any traits in themselves please don't get your knickers in a twist and chill out – it might not be you! But if it is, take it as a compliment.

This is a boy's own adventure story for the twenty first century inspired by the long ago read and remembered comics, books and specially mags. I hope you enjoy my tale as much as I did.

Part One

We're All Going on a Summer Horrorday

I stood looking thoughtfully out of the studio apartment's large beach-facing French window. It was early in the evening, but it was already rather late in May. The spring tide was fully in and the waves looked a little too rough for a paddle. I couldn't help noticing a prominent 'No Dogs' sign, but the couple walking their two hounds didn't look like they gave a shit. Happily, their small terrier looked like he was enjoying his enormously. I'm not normally one to admire the view, or even take the time to look, but I had to admit, Porthmeor Beach was gorgeous, and I started to think about the events that had led me here.

It had been a mild winter, at least the weather had been. Unfortunately, my personal circumstances - what shall we say? Warmed up a little? Getting too hot to handle more like. Anyway, I don't usually bail out at the first sign of trouble, but fuck me, I was feeling a little jaded. I thought a little holiday, maybe the whole of the summer somewhere off the beaten track away from the smoke might do me good. You know the sort of thing, recharge my batteries before a few of the SE7 scallywags tried to refresh my bollocks with their size tens.

Well, you know what they say about the best laid plans!

I had arrived in the back of a black cab early that morning. It had been a bit of a scramble out of the capital, more of a strategic withdrawal really. A couple of heavies representing a couple of even heavier aggrieved gambling buddies didn't quite catch up with me before I skedaddled, thank goodness.

I was tired and unshaven and the near empty bottle of Jack Daniels on my lap balanced precariously as the cab bounced down the hill into St Ives Town. I was still dressed for an evening out in Soho. Bow tie, braces, the lot. I always did look a suave bastard in a monkey suit.

It was nice of the cabbie to 'offer' me a free gratis lift to Cornwall though. Mind you he didn't really know too much about it as I had gazed deeply into his baby blues 'Look into my eyes' and all that hypno-babble did the trick, in fact, he didn't say a dicky bird for three hundred boring miles. Mind you, that's the way I like my cabbages. He was a smallish bald geezer, sweetish boat race, round wire-rimmed glasses, and carrying a few extra pounds. He reminded me a bit of Dr Crippen. Called himself Reuben, at least that's what his name badge said. I guess you could say he was mesmerized, either way he did a sterling job and didn't moan once as I worked my way through twenty smokes while he turned a sickly green pallor. I couldn't help but keep looking at the 'No Smoking' sign on his glass partition. There's always some fucker who wants to spoil the fun!

I dare say his missus went ballistic when he finally got indoors a day late and smelling like an ashtray. I'm sure she'll have had some Febreeze in the cupboard mind. It was probably her made him work the central London nightshift in the first place. Serves her right then I reckon, the greedy cow.

Well, here we were in sunny St Ives, Cornwall. Boutique holiday destination for the more discerning, better earning, arty farty types some might say.

An old pal of mine, nicknamed 'Lucky Lucian', bit of an artist himself by all accounts, owed me a favour. He hadn't been so 'Lucky' lately, well he had just started a six-month holiday of his own to be precise. Regrettably, that's the going rate for getting caught with your pants down and your cock out in a public place these days. Best be discreet if you can't be decent, I always say. Still, it was nice of him to lend me his gaff by the seaside as payment for my help. At least he wasn't going to be mithered and mullered by the other inmates, all thanks to my friendly if not hypnotic chat with the Prison Governor. It's nice to have high friends in low places, ain't that the truth.

As I had butchers out of the cab's side window, I noticed how tropical and clean the manor looked. I flicked my butt accurately out of the window and pleasingly even my discarded empty bottle didn't shatter as it hit the deck on the neatly kept grass verge. Another sign caught my attention. 'Please take your litter home. Thank you!' Thank you, my arse. I hate signs.

The view of the harbour over Reuben's shoulder was breath-taking even if it was through the haze of fag number twenty-one. Yet another piece of street furniture on the side of the road proclaimed, 'Welcome to St Ives, Cornwall.' I remember thinking to myself how nice that was. I would like to think they meant it.

We pulled up outside a largish boozer on the harbour front called The Sloop Inn. It was 6.30am and it was already quite warmish. There were some bench tables outside with a couple of cleaning staff sitting around drinking their first cuppa of the day, while enjoying a crafty drag themselves.

Standing beside Reuben's open window I spoke to him cheerily, although I must admit he looked a little blank. 'Cheers big ears, you must be knackered after all those miles? No? Of course not you've slept all the way haven't you!'

I continued our one-way chat merrily. 'Well, it's been nice doing business with you Reubs, but all good things must come to an end. Normally this is where I would pay you, but I'm afraid I'm gonna have to charge you for the pleasure this time my old son.' He never blinked an eyelid, just handed over his takings through the open window. Two hundred and fifty sovs in crisp tenners.

Pleased as punch, I continued our goodbye one-to-one, 'No, that's too much mate. Here have a score back. You're going to need some gas to get home.' Then, as if I was genuinely concerned I continued, 'I will give you a good tip though Reubs, don't pick up dodgy looking geezers in monkey suits after 2am.' With that I stepped carefully back from the side of the cab. Reuben looked totally oblivious to my humorous asides. 'Off you go then my old cocker,' I said, pointing to the exit road around the side of the pub, 'back to the trouble and strife and the screaming brats. You won't remember a thing about the last five hours I'm afraid so it's all going to be a little bit disconcerting for you.' He never twitched. 'One minute you have just dropped your guts in Piccadilly Square and the next you wake up at the end of the earth, well England anyway.'

He released his handbrake and held the cab on the clutch for a second as I finished my wise words. 'Anyway, just follow the 'All Outbound Traffic' signs and Bob's your uncle and Fanny's your aunt. Don't worry though mate, I've got your number for next time, I'll be in touch. Toodle pip.' I left that thought resonating in his head and with a whiff of diesel fumes, he was gone.

Lighting another fag, I muttered flippantly to myself as the seated staff looked on bemused, 'Chatty bastard!'

Observing the harbour in front of the pub while I smoked, I again admired the view. It really was picture postcard gorgeous. Fuck me, it looked like one of those old railway propaganda posters from the 1930s, you know what I mean I'm sure. 'Come to St Ives, it's as good as Monaco!' Well, it is when it's not pissing down stair rods! The insignia on the pub wall boasted, 'The Sloop Inn – Circa 1312' It was easy to put two and two together and figure the place was probably full of local modern day pirates of an evening, which could of course be rather useful. O'arrrghhhhh!

Well, I didn't have to carry any luggage at least, but I did have the keys to Lucian's studio apartment burning a hole in my back pocket. It was a short trot thankfully, initially up a short nasty slope and I would soon learn that in St Ives you are either going up or going down. The road surfaces are probably not the best either, unless you appreciate a broken ankle that is. I took out the crumpled piece of paper upon which Lucian had scratched down some simple directions. It wasn't long before I was ambling down towards his holiday apartment. It looked fairly bland from the outside, a big front door with two bay windows either side all tucked neatly into the corner of the road. A grey slate-tiled façade and there were even a few plants that looked like they had been looked after with more than a little love in the window boxes on the sandy sills. It was as I entered the small courtyard at the front of the property and turned to close the gate that I noticed a dozen scraggy cats were in tow. There was one large, impressive black brute of a tomcat at the head of them. The thought of the cats, the sea and of using Lucian's little map, and I found myself singing aloud.

Fifteen men on a dead man's chest,

Yo-Ho-Ho and a bottle of rum,

Drink and the Devil have done for the rest.

Errrrrrm, Devil? Better not risk it, didn't want him or any of his mates turning up now, did I? What was needed was a quiet little holiday. Just what the doctor ordered, or would have done, if those bounders from the smoke had gotten hold of me the previous night, I'm sure. My thoughts on entering were, 'This will do nicely my son'.

Closing the door behind me, I glanced back at the cats. They were seated in a line across the road about twenty feet away. Suspecting at the time they were probably scavenging and as I was the only thing moving at that time of day they had probably assumed I was a fisherman and that there were likely to be some scraps to be had.

They couldn't have been that smart though if they believed I was dressed for fishing. Mind you, everything was beginning to smell more than a little bit fishy.

The first thing to do was simply crash out on the king size bed that was all prepared and pristine in the main bedroom. Typical of Lucian the place was, 'Bohemian Boutique' in style and was much more than substantial. The whole gaff was basically fitted out like a large posh loft with three ginormous bedrooms off the one huge living room-cum-dining space. It all had an air of depravity, but was immaculately laid out. The furniture was shabby chic with an emphasis on the chic. Lucian was, after all, never short of the readies.

I must have slept like a log because upon waking and looking at my watch, it was nearly noon. I freshened up and the white freestanding roll-top bath with its chromium fittings was very welcoming as well as aesthetically pleasing. For some probably kinky reason it was placed so you could look out of the large beach facing French window that I had already opened, as it was such a humid day.

The previously pristine bed now looked like Tracey Emin had been bonking frantically on it and there were unfinished paintings scattered all around making the scene look very avant-garde. Alongside the paintings, which seemed to be mainly of naked young men, all in various stages of obscene pose, there were pots of paint and brushes strewn far and wide. It seemed a good bet that Lucian lived the careless, carefree lifestyle when he was down here. Again, I found myself singing aloud as I giggled and soaped my helmet, drawing on my cigarette as if it was my last, which, it actually was.

Fifteen men on a dead man's chest,

Bo-ho-ho and an extremely sore bum!

Catching a view of myself in the full length mirror as I dried myself, I didn't think I looked too bad for thirty-nine. A few grey hairs, but they were lost in my blondish mop of a barnet. The body felt and looked fit and I was in remarkably good shape mentally, for a change. Feeling a niggling rumble in my stomach reminded me, I hadn't eaten for twenty-four hours so redressing firstly in the monkey suit trousers and shirt, I slipped the shoes on but outrageously didn't bother with the socks! Old Lucian was right, this place was magnificent and discreet, only my immediate need was real enough, to get out and about, grab a spot of lunch and purchase some suitable duds with the taxi fund money. Didn't want to stick out like a spare prick at an orgy after all.

Walking back up the slope towards a small shop on the corner of the narrow road I found myself irritated by the dozen or so kitty cats that seemed to want to shadow my every move. The big black tom was clearly the alpha male. Christ, talk about drawing attention to yourself. These fuckers seemed to sense that there was a new king in town and I seriously hoped that nobody else had realised yet.

'Fuck off you bastards!' I yelled at my feline followers. Unfortunately, I hadn't noticed the two young kids with their buckets and spades standing outside the shop doorway. Their accompanying parents were not amused at the outburst, thinking I was yelling inappropriately at their sprogs. The kids were laughing like drains, the cats were scattering and embarrassingly, I apologised to the children's father, 'Sorry gov. I didn't see the nippers.'

Sheepishly entering the shop, it seemed well stocked but a tad claustrophobic. Alert and pert, a poor man's Brigitte Bardot stood behind the counter in a very low-cut T-shirt. The assistant looked better stacked than the shelves and, guessing she was about twenty, there was a familiar twinge in my nether regions. It wasn't just food, fags and clobber that was needed it seemed!

'Hello luv, what time do you get off then?' I inquired.

She smiled back and replied tartly, 'You cheeky beggar, don't you wanna knows my name first like?'

'Plenty of time for that afterwards darlin', I countered. She was grinning from ear to ear as she came from behind the counter. The skirt she had on was as short as the top was low. Standing there with her hands on her hips, one couldn't help but be impressed with how tightly the shop was stocked with everything a man could want. From cornflakes to frozen food, booze, newspapers and, possibly, if she played her cards right, tonight's entertainment.

'I'm Mandy,' she said.

'I bet you are.' I couldn't help myself.

'No silly, thas my name!'

'Well my name's Alexander but you can call me Alex if you like and surely the pleasure will be all mine.'

Mandy blushed hard. 'Better not let my poppa hear you talk like that.'

With a mocking frown I chipped back 'Don't worry luv. What he don't know won't harm him now, will it?'

Mandy looked awkwardly down at the floor. 'He'll do the harming matey if he catches you messing around with me. He broke my last boyfriend's coxis!'

My eyes were watering in sympathy as I replied, 'Ouch! That sounds nasty. He's a real charmer then? Anyhow, do us twenty Super Kings and a bottle of Jack please. That should keep me going till tea-time at least.'

Leaving the shop with Mandy laughing sweetly behind me, I noticed a small hippie chick wearing a large backpack and leaning against the low cold grey granite wall beside the roadside. She had a classy linen jacket, tightly fitted with black leggings and red Doc Marten boots. Her long blonde hair in ringlets made her look prophetically angelic. The cats encircled her feet like disciples and it was obvious to me from the get go what she really was.

I spoke without reverence, but cautiously to her, 'I was wondering how long it would take before one of your sort turned up. Nice bag, always wondered where you hid the wing extensions in the summertime.'

She held my eye and commanded in a sweet but serious tone, 'Follow me conjurer, we need to talk.'

I knew clearly that I didn't have any choice in the matter, so I followed her through the back roads that I was to get to know so well over the next couple of months. The town was like a large maze and as we moved through the main shopping street, she led the way quickly with the large black tomcat ever vigilant at her side, peering occasionally over his shoulder at me, whilst the other moggies spread out amongst the unmindful shoppers. I knew I shouldn't be thinking this about my divine guide, but I couldn't help noticing she had a nice ass.

After ten minutes we arrived at the door of the town's large parish church, Saint EIA. The construction was medieval, over six hundred years old, Anglican with a smattering of cryptic Catholicism and all this dedicated to a Celtic Saint to boot, and very nice she looked too, standing in her Doc Martens in front of the altar.

'I am IA of Cornwall,' she spoke in a kindly voice this time, 'I was carried to this land an age ago. You stand on my grave magician.'

I couldn't help my infantile retort, could I? 'Do you want me to take my shoes off then?'

Her face was beautiful, and she kept her dignity along with her temper as she replied, 'I wish you to behave while you are in my protectorate, Mr Crowley.'

She had apparently done her homework on me then. Who was I to deny an honest-to-goodness real life Twenty-First Century saint?

'Your wish is my command darlin.'

Behind this apparently young girl, was a huge stained glass window depicting her ancient image in a more formal and colourful pose, a silent reminder of her divine authority. Turning slowly to leave, I knew that it was best not to push my luck. I glanced at the font. It had four carved granite angels fixed to its side. They looked like characters frozen in time and I instantly recognised them as clandestine ancient soul prisons and I didn't fancy getting locked in any one of them any time soon. Just before I reached the exit, it was as if my feet were glued to the stone floor. She finished her sermon while I stood annoyed, anchored as her captive audience.

'Do not mock me, Crowley.' She issued her gentle command with style.

Looking at her over my shoulder, now that she had demonstrated her power, it was a simple but obvious question to ask, 'I'm the sinner and you're the saint, is that it?'

'Beyond doubt, Mr Crowley. Beyond doubt.'

Leaving the church, a damn site faster than I had entered, it was noticeable that all the cats had split the scene, except one. The big black tom scrutinized me as I opened a new pack and lit a welcome cigarette while still pondering the conversation with IA. Was she just imparting a little friendly advice or was there more to it? Either way it's not every day you meet a real saint, is it?

Entering the main shopping street which was signed, 'Fore Street', a large surfer dude shop came into view. It was called, 'Unfrequented Pathways'. There was a book shop next door which had a prominent display in its front feature window, promoting a local book. A sizeable poster featuring the book's cover balanced on an artist's easel, 'High on the Tide'. The illustration contained a few pissed-up locals who clearly fancied themselves as some sort of modern-day swashbucklers and they were all bobbing about in an open boat in rather rough seas.

Intrigued, I turned my attention back to the surf shop, entered, and after a quick fillet of the shelves, managed to locate some summer-time attire. Red flip flops, skater shoes, a pair of strides and four T-shirts topped off with a three pack of boxer shorts and a mixture of sport socks. The full fat shop assistant, who looked like someone had stuck a bike pump up his arse and blown his head up, looked rather smug as he tilled the dough. That was the taxi fund gone. Oh well. Easy come, easy go.

The promotional material on show at the bookshop blurted out that the tome was written by resident town novelist, Booby de Faux. There was a picture of him looking superior. He was a cross between Billy Bunter and George Melly. He looked overfed, over refreshed, and over-the-hill and his vibe screamed fat pretentious ex-alcoholic. There was a large tatty trilby balanced on his dome. A middle-aged, not unattractive shop assistant, in a librarian sort of way, all straggly greasy hair and glasses, was putting out a sandwich board on the cobbles outside the bookshop with the legend, 'Author Signing Today, 4pm'.

I carried on walking up the incline with my newly acquired trendy bag of clothes. Glancing back, I saw the black cat and as he passed the advertising board he sprayed it liberally. His piss ran down the authors face onto the cobbles in mock tribute. What kind of character had a name like Booby de Faux I wondered? What the fuck!

It wasn't too long before I was sitting on one of the matching leather armchairs back at the studio apartment drinking a longed-for cup of rosy. Comfortable in my new attire and with my new uninvited companion sat in the corner of the room licking his balls, everything looked and certainly felt at ease and the afternoon sun was pleasantly blazing in through the open glass frontage. The cat was obviously looking after its master's interests, which was cool. I wasn't planning to upset the apple cart, just yet. Peace for once.

It didn't last long as there was a heavy knock at the front door. Not knowing initially what to expect as I opened up, though it definitely wasn't a geezer looking like an out-of-breath fat Doctor Who, all coats, scarf and trilby. He barged past, stinking like a brewery. He hardly glanced around as he cried out theatrically in a rather camp voice, 'Well, well, well, what we have got here then? I take it you are Lucian's new errr, courtesan? Ha, Ha, Ha!' It was more amusing than insulting. Turning about-face, he enquired, 'Is the old fart in? Is he decent, my dear boy?'

I had realised who he was by this point, recognising him from the bookstore display as he carried on mincing around the studio peering into every corner, crying out, 'Lucy baby! Where are you love? Booby's here!'

Squinting as the smoke from my cigarette polluted my eyes, I saw that even the cat had stopped preening himself in astonishment, although he looked on in disgust at the aged public schoolboy with a quizzically angled face.

'Ere, mush!' I exclaimed, 'Lucian ain't here, he ain't decent and if you call me his 'courtesan' again, I'm going to have to give you a serious slap!'

My uninvited guest looked shocked and horrified that a man of his self-importance had been spoken to in such a way. He did, however, apologise immediately and humbly for the assumptions he had made before with such arrogant and insensitive aplomb. 'I, I am sorry young man, I, I thought?' He stumbled to an embarrassed close.

'Yes, I know what you thought,' I countered, moving closer towards him, directing my right index finger at his bulbous red nose, 'You assumed I was your pal's holiday romance. His bum-time fun-time no less!' Standing toe-to-toe with the by now trembling intruder, our heights were the same, but that's where the similarity ended. His gut stopped us getting any closer and the cat went back to licking his balls with some enthusiasm, now he thought the entertainment had peaked.

'Please accept my sincere apologies, I can sense you are a man of virtuous charisma,' he said quivering, dropping his gaze to the floor.

'Don't take the piss pal! Pull up a pew and take that ugly burden off your feet,' I said cruelly.

Sitting opposite each other in the leather armchairs it wasn't long before we were both drinking Lucian's finest whiskey and smoking his best cigars. By this point, the cat had dozed off in the corner, now totally bored to tears with our new found familiarity. It didn't take us long to get acquainted. He seemed a pretentious git, but his heart appeared to be in the right place. He was shocked to hear of Lucian's 'misunderstanding with the law' but a couple more glasses of whiskey and a drag or ten on his Bolivar seemed to mellow his façade.

'Ok. Now we're buddies, who and what exactly are you? I gather you are a writer?'

He hit back immediately, 'Good God man! I am *the* Booby de Faux. Novelist, poet, painter, comedian, actor, raconteur, a critic of some repute! Around these parts anyway. Some say I am good, although the truth be known, I could be better.'

His words trailed off in sadness and his head drooped before I replied,

'Yeah, yeah, yeah, you could have been a contender, right?'

Raising his head heavily and slowly, looking me squarely in the eye, he whispered, 'Not really, too lazy you see. Easier to criticise other more talented artists and God knows, there are enough of them in this town. Even the ones that are dead are more active than yours truly'

In the time it took to visit the sink top to refresh our glasses and return to my chair the black tomcat had awoken and seated himself on my new friend's rather well-padded lap. It seemed that both the cat and I had taken an instant liking to our visitor. His comment about an expired generation of artists had intrigued me, so I thought it best to probe further, 'You're right Mr de Faux. I can feel that there are impressions of the past at play in the town.'

Looking straight at me and with all sincerity, he spoke pleadingly, 'Please call me Booby. I am sure you mean the ghosts, do you not? You are of course right. They are constantly feuding from beyond their graves, just the way they did when they were alive. They have old scores to settle and often they use the local populace as ammunition!'

Offering Booby his replenished glass, the cat bared its fangs at me as my hand traversed its head a little too close for comfort it seemed. 'My name is Alexander Crowley, please call me whatever you like,' I said.

'I'll call you Ally then, if that's all right? It's none of my business, but are you related to err?'

Cutting him short, 'He was my bastard great-grandfather, and I am afraid, the apple hasn't fallen too far from the tree my friend.'

Quizzically, he enquired further 'Bit of a bad egg wasn't he? 666 The Number of the Beast and all that malarkey?'

I thought it best to give him only the family highlights. 'Occultist, magician, poet, painter, novelist, and a bloody good mountaineer to boot, by all accounts.' Booby looked at the snarling cat and with measured insight made another educated statement, 'Looks like our local terrors are aware of your attendance Mr err, Ally. I am even predicting that they may wish to use you to stimulate their little scene given the chance.'

Answering him honestly, I replied, 'It would be best if they left well alone mate. When I get involved, things tend to go sideways at best, tits up at worst. Anyway, chins up. Take me on a tour and fill me in on the gossip. You have a book signing in ten minutes and we wouldn't want to miss that, would we?'

Soon we were walking the back streets through the old town known as 'Downalong' decanting merrily at the beginning of Fore Street. Booby recounted a fascinating and informed potted history of the local culture. At times I found I had my arm around his shoulders as it was oh-so-easy to take an instant shine to my new acquaintance. There were plenty of early season tourists about, along with buskers, artists with their mobile easels and even a human statue painted silver with top hat, Steam Punk in style.

The adjectives flew from Booby as he clearly had great affection for all things artistic in St Ives. Some of the characters he mentioned were known to me, such as Dame Barbara Hepworth, Ben Nicholson, Lucian Freud, Mark Rothko, Bernard Leach and Sir Terry Frost. Others were held somewhere in the back of my mind like Peter Lanyon, Troika Pottery, Sandra Blow,

Hamada, Alfred Wallis, Naum Gambo and the SS Alba. Further names were mentioned that meant absolutely nothing to me at this stage, Sir Anthony Kingston, Portreeve John Payne, The Tate Gallery and the intriguingly named sculptor, Sven Berlin. All the time we walked, talked and laughed our way along Fore Street, we were shadowed by the black cat, never more than a dozen paces away. Cats, it seemed, made the perfect spies, but this one was not discreet or indeed secretive. His presence was surely a reminder to behave myself. Not much chance of that, I thought. Saying farewell to Booby, I was sure to see him later on as he bounded into the bookshop and his waiting audience, which seemed to consist sadly, only of the staff.

After a short wander I took a seat on the stone steps of the town's War Memorial and lit what was again alarmingly, my last fag, in that packet anyway. The cat looked on with loathing as the empty packet bounced discarded onto the road. Strangely, he appeared to be guarding me now, even though he seemed to detest litter louts. Booby sure knew his local folklore, but it was about time to make some of my own. When in need I'm afraid I am always willing to do a dirty deed. The taxi cash was gone, so it was understandable where my next visit would be. The bank.

Walking up the High Street slope past the Golden Lion public house and there it was, salvation. 'Free Cash' it declared on the ATM fascia and that's exactly what I had in mind. Observation was always one of my strengths and being as how it's often the downfall of the majority of the population, I had always made a good living from my dubious skill.

An old lady overdressed in a heavy winter coat, Hilda Ogden headscarf and balancing herself precariously with the help of her ancient shopping trolley, was openly tapping in her pin number. 1-2-3-4, not very original, but all very convenient for me at least. I bumped gently into her shoulder, spinning her around like a top as I meandered by. I'm sure the scene would have looked innocent enough to any passer-by. 'Oops! Sorry luv. Wasn't paying enough attention,' I said, as I caught her and more importantly, her bank card, before they could both hit the deck, then holding her under her arms, I helped her get her balance. 'No harm done dear,' I suggested as I locked her into a simple daydream. She was very frail so I should have been sickened by my own behaviour. You can imagine though, there had been a whole lot worse than this in the past.

Escorting and encouraging the old lady across the road towards the café was easy, and although she was flushed and disorientated, she looked relieved when I sat her down inside and ordered her a nice cup of tea to steady her nerves. 'There you go darlin', have a moment there. You'll be as good as new in a minute.'

It's always best to use the cash point card that's issued by the same bank holding the account I find. Always a higher withdrawal limit you see, and I was gladdened to find out she was a loyal saver. Four hundred pounds in one go was more than useful for a couple of days expenses and no CCTV either to give the game away. Once the notes were counted and I had pocketed my ill-gotten gains, I glanced over at the old lady sitting inside the café. She was enjoying her surprise refreshment and I noticed she had added a tea cake, so it hadn't all been bad news for her that afternoon, had it?

Off again and on further up the High Street, passing a holiday agents shop called St Ives Breaks. Two large screens in the feature window were showing extracts of holidaymakers having a grand old time, frolicking about on the beaches and judging by the advertised prices, it was doubtful whether they could have afforded to do anything else during their stay!

Around the right hand corner at the top of the High Street and I was in a rather dingy looking backstreet which was full of takeaways. I took the time to pause and survey the scene. A Chinese called, 'The Suzy Sue', a Kebab Shop which looked filthy and that I immediately thought to christen, 'The Chew and Spew', an Indian restaurant called, 'The Khyber Pass', whilst a number of other adjacent properties were boarded up, it seemed even a little paradise like St Ives had its less salubrious areas.

At the far end of the road was a pub. There were a few scruffy looking locals standing outside, smoking and trying to look hard while a sign over the door proclaimed an unlikely, 'The Bizz'. Looking behind me, my feline friend was off, returning to his saintly boss to grass me up no doubt. Either that or this place really must have been as rough as Booby had intimated. Nevertheless, it was the table sportsmen inside that I was interested in. Entering the boozer it was as if someone had turned the sun off. You could make out a pool table slap bang in the middle of the long half-full room and there were a couple of beaten up bandits, a cigarette machine and a dartboard that looked as if someone had been throwing machetes at it. The afternoon clientele would have been best described as, 'scrotes', not to put too fine a point on it.

I had carried on smoking my cigarette upon entry, as I had never liked to encourage the Licensing Laws to spoil my own personal enjoyment. 'You can't smoke in 'ere chummy.' The deep, menacing noise came from a big fat ugly bastard who was seated in the left hand corner of the bar at a table on his own. He had an empty collection of pint pots in front of him.

'Says who?' I inquired sarcastically.

As he leant forward onto his elbows into the light, I gauged him to be about six foot four and north of two hundred and fifty pounds of blubber and muscle. 'I do, you tosser!' he exclaimed, obviously getting more than a little excitable.

'And who, pray are you my man?' Thinking back, it was probably this comment that upset the apple-cart. He truly was a bit of a poor man's behemoth. He jumped clumsily to his feet, knocking over the table and sending the glasses crashing and smashing to the floor.

'I'm your worsetest nightmare, wankstain!' he shouted.

The other drinkers made space in preparation for a John Wayne fight scene. I stubbed my cigarette out on the stone floor with arrogant calm, and I don't know why I said it, but I couldn't help myself, 'Don't make me take my coat off, fatty. There's no need for fisticuffs!'

With that, he exploded into action, but as he threw his first and only punch, I ducked low and helped my assailant with a well-trained shoulder to deposit his weight heavily and, more importantly, painfully onto a filthy looking table top. The table buckled around his monstrous frame with a terrific crash and one of the legs conveniently caught him a nasty blow to the temple as he collapsed in a heap, unconscious. I think the local clientele were suitably impressed as blood started to gush from a nasty looking cut on the fat man's head. Lighting a fresh cigarette, I chattered aloud, 'Tut, tut, tut, clumsy clot!'

From the side of the bar, a tall, elegant man appeared out of the gloom. He looked to be in his fifties with greying temples and was dressed in some style with waistcoat complete with fob watch and chain. The words 'flashy' and 'superior' came to mind. He reminded me of a thin George Clooney. I couldn't help think that the pool cue he held in his right hand, had clearly nothing to do with a game he had been playing, although, he did look like he had just potted the winner. He exclaimed, 'Bravo! Bravo!'

'You're the real gaffer here then?' I enquired.

'Well deduced my friend,' he replied, 'Mr Bucca Dhu at your service.' The accent was formal sinister.

'Charmed I'm sure, Alexander… Alexander Crowley.' We stood opposite each other, as a couple of local struggling sycophants assisted the fat man to his knees.

'Maybe we could retire to my office, Mr Crowley? Surely we have things to discuss? Perhaps a little refreshment?' He sounded almost genuine.

'Thank you,' I replied, 'that would be delightful.'

A few minutes later we were sat opposite each other, either side of a large office desk in Mr Bucca Dhu's private office. The whiskey he provided was first rate and I'd like to think I can tell the difference. The room was contemporary in style, very tidy, but devoid of natural light. The single exit put me slightly on edge, as we sat illuminated by the low yellowish light emitted from the overhead Art Deco light bowl fitting.

'That was very impressive the way you dealt with my errrm, attendant Mr Crowley. He is normally more than a match for any of the town's revellers and riff raff.' I noticed he never blinked once as he spoke and held my stare.

'Don't be too hard on him. I'm sure he is better than useful under normal circumstances,' I suggested in jest.

He leant forward topping up our drinks and continued calmly 'It's your uses I am more interested in Sir. I am aware of your celebrity. Certainly we could come to some sort of mutual agreement. Who knows, maybe even a profitable business arrangement?'

I couldn't help smirking as I lowered my empty glass to the desk.

'I sensed what was going on here and who you were Mr Dhu about ten seconds after the cat took off for the hills. I don't normally do deals with the devil or his close associates, so don't try and take me for a mug.'

I covered the glass with my hand to discourage another top up and continued, 'So, you can drop the pretence as well as the cloak. I can see you for what you really are and I can assure you, I'm not scared of minor league demons.'

Bucca Dhu laughed politely and a Jekyll to Hyde transformation took place all within a second or two. His real demonic appearance was pretty standard, a black spirit with smallish horns, a long pointed nose and lidless eyes. He managed to look fairly menacing, but didn't intimidate me overly. After all, I'd seen this type of morphing many times, mind you never before at my own request.

'Very well magician, have it your way, it is always wonderful to dispense with the niceties.' His voice had dropped an octave lower than before.

'Nothing nice about you mate. Your punters would shit their pants if they could see you now,' I japed.

Bucca Dhu sniggered craftily at my response and then came straight to the point.

'Of course you are right, hah, hah! Now, how can we trade?'

Slinging my feet up onto his desk to let him understand who was boss, I stated the facts as I saw them. 'It's all about needs, yes? I'm going to need some cash to live the life and you of course need to cause a little misery. Purely for your own enjoyment I would imagine?'

Bucca Dhu turned slowly sideways on his chair so as not to look me directly in the eye.

'You are correct, my clever friend, although I do have a nuisance in town that I am sure you can relieve me of. In fact, I can guarantee you will profit handsomely from your efforts, with my help of course.'

I was intrigued, but wary. Leaning forward, my cigarette smoke spiralled upwards under the yellow beam. 'Tell me more Mr Dhu, one man's nuisance is another man's nuance, or so they say.'

I never claimed to be a social worker, however, it's always interesting to hear about other folk's problems. Seemed my new evil buddy had a beef with the local head honcho who was oppressing and ruling the town with the assistance of his hired muscle. Most of his funds came from traditional and varied immoral business ventures and sources associated.

Apparently, this geezer had two major weaknesses. Firstly, he liked a drink and secondly, he loved to gamble in Bucca Dhu's boozer, showing off to his crew. Of course, he who holds the cash is king. Well, I thought to myself, there's a new king in town now and it wasn't the monster sat opposite.

As I left The Bizz, I spotted the wounded fat man perched on an undersized, well at least for his frame, stool just outside the entrance door. He was being supported by a couple of bootlicker buddies and was rubbing his newly bloodied head. I flicked my kaput cigarette butt his way as a generous leaving present and this time he knew better than to complain about my manners.

A few paces into the street and my mind was whirling, considering the rest of Bucca's story. The local Cornish Mafioso was called Lillo Contattio. Stereotypically, he was of Italian descent, short, stocky and full of malice. An unusual, eclectic mix, though he apparently loved his ice cream and cappuccino as long as there was a hint of mackerel about it! He also cherished a game of poker on a Saturday night and tonight Matthew, as they say, I was going to be a latter day Doc Holiday. Seemed the best way to hurt him was in the pocket. The next best way was family and even now I was unintentionally working on that, having already met his buxom daughter, Mandy.

Back on Fore Street, it was early evening now and there waiting to pick up my pursuit where he had left off, sitting in the church entry was the handsome black cat.

So, it was to be a fairly simple arrangement. Bucca Dhu had supplied me with some serious betting money and I was going to join the Saturday night card game as his surprise guest. The police were going to be waiting close at hand for when it all kicked off and matey boy Contattio would be on his way to a padded cell faster than a rat up a drainpipe. The gangster's posse would then be inherited by the demonic Mr Dhu and he would seamlessly take over the Cornish Mafioso's dubious business interests. Sounded like a good plan to me the more I thought about it. Bucca got the run of the town's illegal ops and I got the cash and some girly action. All this without getting my head staved in with a bit of luck. Super-duper!

Only one real problem came to mind, IA. She wouldn't be too impressed, I was sure. But hey-ho, the devil drives and all that hokum, so I put the thought conveniently to the back of my mind.

The teatime kip was welcome, but it wasn't long before there was a knock on the studio apartment door. As I stood in my boxers at the entrance, Booby rushed in past me transporting a formal black suit on a hanger. He also had an immaculately pressed white shirt over his other arm complete with skinny black tie and he held a pair of the shiniest black Oxfords by their inserted shoehorns, I had ever seen. 'These should do nicely Ally. Probably last wore them ten years and ten stone ago at Francis's funeral. I was certainly the debonair man about town back then.'

Soon the suit was fitted to my frame, all with Booby's over-attentive assistance, 'You were a bit keen on the inside leg there my old son,' I cracked. 'Wrong side though Boob's, I always dress to the right, adds a little confusion to the proceedings.' He couldn't help laughing sheepishly as he confirmed I looked like the veritable 'West Country James Bond'.

We were soon out on the back road making our way to our 9.30pm kick off. It was fairly dark by now and there were only a few holidaymakers milling about, aimlessly looking into retail windows. Mandy Contattio stood in her shop doorway, hands on hips, looking rather put out. As we passed on by, I threw a comment over my shoulder, 'Don't wait up darlin. I'll catch you later on if you're lucky.' I didn't catch her reply, but it seemed quite short and to the point.

Booby looked like the cat had got the cream as he escorted me onwards through Fore Street, pretending shamelessly to be my date. The black cat followed at an inconspicuous distance and although I was beginning to take a shine to him, I do remember thinking what a nosy bastard he was, and when we finally turned off the High Street, he once again sensibly took a pew in one of the boarded-up doorways, as if to say, 'See you later boys'.

We approached The Bizz with panache at least, though plenty of the local scrotes around the entrance were sneering at my dress code, plus my now nervous companion had started sweating profusely in his coat, scarf and trilby. We must have looked like James Bond and Doctor Who out on the piss. The fat man was sitting on his favourite stool outside the front entrance sporting a nice new bandage on his head, all set off beautifully with the most horrendous black eye. 'Looks nasty mate. Accident was it?' I inquired then followed up maliciously with, 'Try not to have another one hey?'

He remained sensibly seated, seething with hatred as another tall scruff in a Breton striped t-shirt, top hat and eye patch for good measure, directed us towards a side door just inside the pub's entrance. He reminded me of a cheaper version of a Claridge's doorman, though he certainly didn't smell like one. We were guided rather than escorted down the short hallway. The passage was dimly lit again in a yellow hue from the one naked bulb hanging from the high ceiling. Booby was looking over his shoulder all the time, although I don't know what he intended to do if we were rushed. The tall scrote opened the door at the end of the passage which revealed a large sitting room with a hefty oblong table centrally placed and six seated men present. Well, five and a demon to be more precise.

Bucca Dhu was sat majestically in a green leather captain's chair, clearly the host with the most, while beside him was a squat looking geezer decked out in the full gangster chic. Pinstriped whistle, kipper tie plus the obligatory scar running from his forehead to his top lip. Luckily it didn't spoil his looks. Mr Lillo Contattio in the flesh, and he certainly made mine crawl. There were four other players installed around the table, local bigwigs presumably, smartly turned out and all subservient to the brooding gangster. The tall fellow, who had shown us in, took up his position behind and to one side of his mobster boss and another scrote clone, already in attendance wearing the identical modern day pirate get-up as his pal, slotted in at the other side. It was also a little alarming to see two huge Rottweilers off the lead sitting against the wall at the back of the room, keeping their eyes on Contattio's every move, seemingly desperate for his instructions. The scene looked full on gambling den kosher, with bottles of whiskey and vodka cluttering up the table top along with a multitude of ashtrays. Everybody seemed to have two glasses and it was clear that there was not a smoking ban in force, as the atmosphere was like a fart filthy sauna.

The large clock on the wall said 10pm and Bucca Dhu was the first to speak.

'You are late Mr Crowley.'

'Got here as soon as I could, my old mate,' I replied as I sank into the vacant chair opposite the cloaked demon, 'I'm sure it will be worth these gentlemen's wait Mr Dhu.'

'Of that I am sure Mr Crowley. You have the funds to play I take it?'

It was a nice touch him asking, of course, considering it was he who had staked me so generously in the first place.

'Is this enough?' I placed a large wad of cash down on the table, pulled from my right inside jacket pocket. It wouldn't have taken my companions long to work out that there was upward of ten grand in front of me on the table. I placed my other hand, in the opposite side of my jacket and slowly pulled out a replica pile. A few of the players looked at each other in concern, but obviously pleased to see my intent.

'Deal the cards, broken nose,' I quipped.

'Very funny Mr Crowley,' my host replied wearily.

He split the deck, the dogs seemed to relax, the gangster's two attendants stepped back a little and we were off to a gentle enough start at least. The first half dozen hands were light-weight and everyone was about even. My third cigarette of the session was lit after an hour by Booby who had been sitting on a spare chair, frightened and yet fascinated, against the wall behind me. I threw my fifty pound stake in and Bucca Dhu dealt each of us five cards. It was just gone 11pm and Contattio was getting a little trigger happy and restless it appeared. Once he had reviewed his cards he threw in two hundred pounds, his arrogant way of letting everyone know that he was the main man. I couldn't see much of a likeness between him and his daughter Mandy, thank goodness, as his fat, pockmarked, greasy face was enough to put anybody off their vinegar stroke.

The evening ground on and was going to plan, my plan that was. At about midnight Contattio was starting to get rather irritated seeing as his preliminary cash pile had been halved. So had most of the bottles and it was fair to say that five of the seven players were a tad pissed. Booby had dropped off to sleep and looked rather uncomfortably propped up in the corner. Contattio spoke for the first time as he barked out to one of his attendants, 'Fill me up Flotsam!' His voice was gruff and strangely Cornish considering his Mediterranean appearance.

The lanky streak of piss meandered over gingerly and with a tepid, 'Yus sir boss,' leant over his chief's shoulder and as he topped the glass up, nearly choked to death on the gangster's cigar fumes.

As he withdrew, coughing his heart out, I pointed unwholesomely at the other attendant who had yet to move a muscle and enquired, 'Don't tell me the other muppet's Jetsam, right?'

Contattio's face reddened and he disrespectfully replied, 'Thas very astute of you Mr Crawley.'

'It's Crowley actually,' I snapped back, 'As in the big black bird... lard head, but you can call me Alexander.'

Contattio was up on his feet immediately, spitting his cigar out in disgust. Both Flotsam and Jetsam had his back and I couldn't help notice the previously concealed long bladed knives they had pulled out into the open. Bet they were good at filleting fish, but luckily Bucca Dhu intervened, just in the nick of time, 'Gentlemen! Gentlemen! There is no need for any unpleasantness over a simple misunderstanding,' he placed his arm across Contattio's chest in a gentle restraining stance, 'Let's play cards huh? We can err, socialise later.'

At least the commotion had woken Booby who had splutter-choked himself back into the real world with all the commotion. 'Amen brother,' I chipped in mockingly. The game had carried on undisturbed now for what seemed an age. A glance at the wall clock confirmed it was 1.25am. The atmosphere was heavy with smoke and tension and the Cornish Al Capone was clearly now well past his sell-by-date. His pallor was a true reflection of the sewage he had ingested during the evening and this was my opportunity to take him for the fool he really was. Leaning forward I caught his eye. With a glint in mine and a little further concentration on my half, it was only a couple of seconds until I had him locked under my control. This sort of hypnotism is dangerous for both parties, yet he hadn't got the gumption to grasp what was happening to him, so he didn't put up any resistance to my hypno-spell.

Bucca Dhu was expecting my move I'm sure, and knew immediately what had occurred. I bet he was enjoying the moment sickeningly to the full.

Contattio's face contorted into a grimace. He looked like he had just been shot, which in a manner of speaking, he had been. Giving him a cheeky wink, I spoke to him under my breath, 'Got yer! You fat fuck!'

We played a couple more games until it was obvious to me, that no one had suspected foul play, the clock was now a little past 2am. The hand, we had been playing had built up nicely and the pot was bulging. Only Contattio and I were left in and I decided that this was to be the final decisive hand. Looking directly at the mesmerized hood I said, 'Let's say we make this a bit more interesting my old cocker?' I removed a further four tidy wads of cash from my seemingly bottomless inside jacket pockets. Fifty grand in fifty-pound notes in total. The other players murmured amongst themselves;

I suspect glad to be out of the game. I leaned in a little further as I tightened the mental grip on the gangster's psyche and ventured, 'It's gonna cost you fifty grand to see me, my son. Reckon that will make the pot two hundred and fifty thousand in all. It's shit or bust big man!'

Contattio's face was now blank as he looked slowly at the five cards he held in his stubby, grubby left hand. Sluggishly, he turned and spoke to his sweaty minder in a monosyllabic tone, 'Errrr, give me the float Jetsam.'

The startled hoodlum replied slowly, 'Are yuh sure boss?'

Contattio nodded his head lethargically and Jetsam obviously decided it was not in his best interest to pursue the matter any further. Jetsam was also further assured that his boss knew what he was doing as he had seen his cards. A full house, three Aces and two Kings, clearly he rightly supposed, the winning hand. I, on the other hand, had a two of hearts, a five of spades, a nine of clubs, a four of diamonds and the inevitable Ace of spades. Ace high, or as they say in other less educated parts, fuck all!

The gangster was now tamer than a sloth on sleeping pills as he laid his fifty grand down on top of the messy pile of cash already deposited. You could have heard a pin drop as all the other players looked on in trepidation. It was as if the moment had been frozen in time. Holding Contattio within my stare, I asked, offering mock transparency, 'Well, I guess you want to see my hand then my old mucker?'

Contattio twitched and blinked as he replied much to everyone's amazement, 'Nuh, no that's alright Alexander. I know when I am beaten. I err, trust you.'

I could see Bucca Dhu smiling slyly out of the corner of my eye. Booby was aghast and the rest of the roomsters were dumbfounded. Contattio looked satisfied when I complimented him like the obedient dog he had become, 'There's a good boy then.'

Booby helped scoop up the winnings and the cash was shovelled into a rather tatty looking plastic carrier bag. That was the end of the night's sport as far as I was concerned and time indeed to depart before the Cornish mobster came fully to his senses.

Bish, Bash, Bosh. Adios losers!

As we reached the far end of the street I lit two cigarettes and my nervous friend, and I watched in amusement and a little horror whilst we smoked, at the devastation unfolding behind us. The scene to the front of the pub was lit by a few street lamps and the light coming from a couple of the takeaways that were still surprisingly open at this late, unsociable hour. Police sirens were wailing and the boys in blue were piling in en masse through the front doors, as most of the furniture seemed to be coming out of the windows into the road. There were shards of glass everywhere and it was with some hilarity, I saw the seated fat man coshed mercilessly by a young enthusiastic police constable. The sound of truncheon on skull was disappointingly muted by the full bandage already in place.

Do-Dah-Do-Dah-Do-Dah. Crash! Bang! Wallop!

Seems Contattio had woken from his trance with a vengeance!

It was clear that Booby was frightened and wanted to go home so I turned around, beckoned the cat from where we had left him and we made our way merrily from the ensuing mayhem. The boys in blue were having a great time. You can't normally find a copper when you want one. Not a bad night all in all. Plenty of funds for the summer once I had settled with the demonic Mr Bucca Dhu and as the night was still young, I thought I might go and see if I could knock Mandy up. If you know what I mean!

Part Two

Two Birds in One Stone

I always enjoyed Sunday mornings, best part of the week, although I had often spoilt it with the most appalling hangovers. At first it wasn't obvious to me, whether the banging was inside my head or not, but the persistent rapping must be knuckle on wood.

'Hold your horses Booby! Is your arse on fire or something?' But when I opened the door IA stood there looking ever radiant although clearly infuriated, so got my apology out quickly. 'Errm, sorry luv, I thought you were Booby.' Ignoring me, the saint just marched straight into the studio uninvited. She was dressed exactly the same as the last time I saw her, all leggings and Doc Martens. The way she always wore the backpack, secured tightly by both shoulder straps, was a reminder of what she really was, and I didn't want to see her wings extended because I figured they might appear at the same time she would probably be sticking the boot in. The ever-present black cat purred contemptuously as he followed her in, hot on his mistress's heels.

Standing there with only my colourful boxers on, I turned to see where my guest had halted. She stood glaring into the master bedroom at the large double bed upon which the naked Mandy Contattio was draped, fast asleep and full of my sin. Clothes were scattered haphazardly about the floor.

The saint spoke with her back to me. 'I know who you thought I was magician, though sodomy and poor taste in clothes are not among my earthly sins.'

'I better put the kettle on then, shall I?'

At first I thought Mandy must have been the type to sleep through a train crash, but I soon figured out that she would not wake until the saint allowed it. I placed the two cups down on the floor between the leather armchairs and sat opposite IA like a naughty school child. It would have been about 11.30am I reckoned, so I must have missed Sunday worship, but I didn't think for one moment that that was the reason she was so annoyed. Moving gracefully to the edge of her seat, she held up her right hand displaying her tiny fingers. I didn't dare risk a high five in reaction.

'Five of the seven deadly sins,' she started, 'Lust, Greed, Sloth, Wrath and Envy.'

Smiling nervously I replied, 'Well, I'm glad you haven't got me down for the other two at least. Pride and Gluttony I believe?'

IA's expression was dignified. 'Correct, magician. Gluttony, not as yet and Pride, albeit of another context, may be somewhat lacking in your genes I suspect.'

Well, that was OK then! Taking a sip of my tea, I asked, 'You sound a little disappointed darlin', is it something I've done?' I expected her wings to appear and the feathers to fly at that last crack.

IA stood bolt upright and though in this human form she was only petite, her presence was that of a giant. Although she didn't need the support, the cat had also moved alongside her and looked as if he fancied a pop, even if she didn't.

'I will trade you your five sins for three of the seven virtues Mr Crowley,' she said, finishing her sentence while pointing at the sleeping Mandy Contattio, 'otherwise, she will never wake again.'

'Hey! That's a bit heavy!'

'Charity, Kindness and Humility,' she continued.

I knew I wasn't in any position to argue.

'Alright. It's a deal, what exactly do you want me to do?'

Put simply, I really had no choice.

Thirty minutes later and it was me doing the knocking for a change. This time it was on the front door of a small, terraced cottage in amongst the back streets of Downalong. The irony wasn't wasted on me as I stood in the quaintly, saintly named St EIA Street. The front door opened slowly and there stood the little old lady I had robbed at the ATM the previous day. She was very frail and looked a little confused by my appearance, looking through me rather than at me. It didn't come naturally, yet even I couldn't argue with a saint's logic, so I introduced myself, 'Hello luv, remember me from yesterday? I've got a present for you. Can I come in please?'

Not really waiting for an invite, I squeezed my way past her as she trawled her memory whilst my feline minder followed me through to a small and extremely cluttered sitting room. Finding out quickly that her name was Edith, it wasn't long before we were drinking out of the best bone china and tucking into a packet of chocolate digestives. My boat race was unmistakably familiar to her, only I'm not sure she could really place me, thank goodness. The cottage was as clean as a whistle, probably because it didn't host too many visitors. It seemed that the husband had shuffled off this mortal coil fifteen years earlier and her only daughter had moved up country not long afterwards, to be seen only at Christmas and on Edith's birthday which, unfortunately, was on January the second. Sadly, once a year, then, was the duty call going rate. It also came up in conversation that she seemed to have lost her savings while she had been out shopping the day before. It was the last four hundred pounds, she had in the world and to put it bluntly, she hadn't got a pot to piss in.

'Never mind, Edith,' I offered, 'That's why I've come here to see you today. I won't tell you a lie, it was me who stole your money. Yes, I know, it was evil of me, but I was down on my luck and desperate you see.' Her tiny face looked horrified at my confession so I continued mock abashed, 'I am sincerely ashamed of myself girl and I hope you can find it in your sweet heart to forgive me.'

Well, that was the humility done, now it was time for the painful bit so, removing a large A4 brown envelope from my inside pocket, I placed it down in front of her on the parlour table. 'It wasn't enough for me to just steal from you Edith. Then, scoundrel that I am, I went straight to the bookies and put the whole lot on some nags that my mate had tipped me off about earlier.' I have no idea if she believed or even understood this nonsense I was spreading on so thickly, but I waded through to the punchline regardless.

'Anyway darlin', I had the most unlikely treble come in at outrageous odds and it's only right I split the winnings with you isn't it?'

Charity and kindness in one go or to be more accurate, 10K down the swanny!

Soon, standing out on the cobbles, placing a goodbye kiss on Edith's cheek, I felt that at least the danger I had placed Mandy in had been neutralised. The cat blew me out fast enough though, and the sneaky bleeder took off down the hill toward the church, evidently keen to confirm my repentance with his guvnor. I remember thinking that if he didn't vouch for me now, after what I had just done out of the kindness of my heart, I'd be sticking a banger up his arse and celebrating Guy Fawkes Night a little earlier this year.

Coming back through the door of the studio apartment I was pleasantly relieved to see Mandy standing at the cooker frying up a late breakfast. She was wearing a short skirt and T-shirt, no shoes and, more noticeably, no bra.

'Where you been my luver? 'she inquired cheekily.

I didn't answer preferring to slump into one of the armchairs.

'I've been up for ages. How do you like your eggs? Fried boiled or poached?' It was a simple enough sort of question from a simple enough sort of woman. The type I wasn't of course used to, or could appreciate.

The dining table I noticed had been formally set and the condiments were laid out neatly so it was a safe bet to assume that she was also skilled in the ways of a silver service waitress. Mandy lowered the hot plate down onto a seascape place mat and stood the mug of tea next to it for company.

It wasn't kind of me to speak to her like I did, only my rough upbringing reared its head once again as I spat out, 'Getting a bit presumptuous for a one night stand aren't you darlin'?'

'You didn't call me that when you was knocking at the shop door at four in the morning did you? You was beggin' me then! I was your bestest girl ever, I think you said!'

'Yeah, yeah, yeah, whatever!'

The rest of Sunday passed off pleasantly enough.

I always did enjoy a beach picnic. I also craved a bit of hush and I wasn't getting much of that as Mandy flitted and fart-arsed about the large beach towel we were decamped upon. She was more out of her yellow polka dot bikini than she was in it and the sun was searing. It wasn't quite midday yet and she hadn't stopped talking for hours. 'Good job Monday's me day off Alex,' she piped up cheerfully.

'Yeah, triffic,' I replied sarcastically. I had only known her a day or so, but she was getting on my tits already.

She drew her large sunglasses down from her eyes so she could no doubt admire me in my shorts while she continued to prittle prattle, 'My dad had a bit o'bother last night it seems. My mum is really upset, he didn't come home like. Do you know anything about it Alex?'

'Unfortunately not darlin',' I lied.

The glasses were slid back up her nose, yet the mouth was still going ten to the dozen, 'Mind you Alex, it's beautiful for May innit?'

I wished I could have closed my ears as tight as my eyes. She was right however, it was beautiful and although she was a sweet kid, I unkindly wished she was back at work. Mandy must have realised I was trying to have a kip and ceased the rabbit, but no sooner had she stopped yacking, I felt the temperature drop as something large cast its unwelcome shadow over my lily-white body.

'Hello sailor!' came the cry. 'Guess who?' It was, of course, Booby.

'Don't block the sun out Boobs, there's a good lad.'

He moved to the side huffily.

'Oh! Bitchy bitch, who's got out of bed the wrong side then?'

Booby flopped down next to Mandy on the towel and they both immediately burst out laughing at my cantankerous demeanour.

Leaving the two of them chuckling like a couple of seasoned up hyenas, I made a pathway across the beach towards the Island, a rocky outcrop on the eastern side of the beach. Before I got out of earshot, I heard Mandy speak acidically, 'Said he wanted a bit o'space,' to which Booby replied, 'Blokes like him always want a bit of space, dearie,' before they continued with their giggling. They were, of course, both correct.

It was a peninsula, not an island, as it was only surrounded by sea on three sides. It was famous only as a location for the much-lamented Radio 1 roadshow back in the 70's. At its summit and only a small distance from a coast watch station, stood a tiny chapel. St Nicholas was a simple place which I imagined would have doubled up as a good lookout, as well as a place of worship in more confrontational times. Approaching the doorway, a little breathless after the climb, it wasn't surprising to see the black tomcat sitting nonchalantly in the chapel's doorway. Inside, IA was seated on the small centrally placed table, her legs swinging free like a young child awaiting a birthday present. This time, for a change, she was kitted out in a long summer dress and sandals, looking every inch the holidaymaker. She must have been confident that we would not be disturbed, as her backpack was lying open on the stone floor, and I could make out her wings neatly tucked in at her sides. I noticed a couple of votive candles burning lonely on the ledge beneath the main window that looked out to sea.

Lighting a cigarette, I inhaled deeply, as IA looked up and spoke first.

'You knew I was here Mr Crowley?'

I knew alright, don't ask me how, yet I knew. Call it instinct, hallowed sites had always held an attraction for me and talking about attractions, God, she was gorgeous. She was probably deadly as well and although it was hard not to like her, I thought it best to keep our relationship strictly professional. I like an older woman, but a fifteen-hundred-year age gap could have been a problem and her being dead, strictly speaking, wouldn't have helped either.

I pointed at the cat while pocketing my lighter in false bravado with my other hand.

'Sorry about the other night and all that again, but I'm sure your friend there has brought you up to speed with my good deeds?'

I thought I caught her smile as she replied, 'Indeed, our settlement is complete for now magician, although I feel it would be best for us to strike a treaty.' Stepping down gently from the table, her wings were a little more visible as she caught her balance.

'A treaty? Why?' I enquired.

'You will not be left alone or at peace in this town without my assistance, Mr Crowley. Your presence will be like a magnet for ne'er do wells, both human and other,' she warned.

I didn't think humans would be too much of a problem for me, but I took her point seriously about the 'others' without fully understanding what that could really mean. The saint extended her wings flatteringly and they filled the chapel physically as they filled me with awe. Christ! I thought, talk about getting them out for the lads!

Once she had finished her stretch she continued on from her warning, 'There are works I cannot do personally about my parish that nonetheless need undertaking and you shall be my conduit, Mr Crowley. In return I will become your custodian.'

I would never have imagined I'd need a saint as a minder, although if you couldn't trust an angel to tell the truth, who could you trust? So, I took her offer gladly at face value. The cat farted rudely for effect as I passed him on the way out of the chapel and it wasn't long before I was again on the beach walking back to my two newfound friends.

It wasn't a date as such, only IA had told me to meet her at midnight at another church up another hill, Treggana Hill to be precise. Fancy being so popular that, regardless of the spelling, you had two churches named after you in the same town. This one was called The Sacred Heart and St IA, so she was sharing top billing this time. That's Catholics for you, I guess!

My reflection bounced back at me from Mandy's large sunglasses.

'Oh! You come back then.'

I lit a fresh cigarette, took a deep breath and bit back hard.

'You can cut the mardy out Mands. We ain't married, in fact we ain't anything!'

That clearly hurt her, and she stormed off with tears streaming down her cheeks while Booby looked on stunned. She left her parting shot hanging in the air.

'You bastard! You wait till I tell my poppa!'

I mused that she would have to wait till visiting time at Bellmarsh to have that conversation and that was a bit of a jaunt from down here. Mind you, it was her old man's fault for being a 'Category A Psycho'. Only time that arsehole got a straight A in his life I chuckled to myself.

Booby was now looking a tad po-faced and from his seated spectator's position held his nose in the air as he commented, 'There was no need to treat her like that Ally, she seems like such a nice girl.'

Initially looking shamefully down at the sand between us, as his comments were of course spot on, then raising my head and regarding him directly, I advised, 'Lovely or not, she's better off out of it mate, I am doing her a favour as things might get a little fractious from here-on-in.'

Midnight, always a good time to do a bit of business, as normally there are no nosey fuckers about. So there I was, sat on a granite bench smoking peacefully just off Treggana Hill at the side of the church whilst listening to the bells of St EIA's ringing in the distance, wondering of course, why my saintly minder had wanted to meet me here in the first place.

I didn't have long to wait as on the twelfth clang of the distant bell, IA descended in flight from above, looking like a mixture of Joan of Arc and a golden eagle. She wore full Celtic battle armour, and I couldn't help notice the alarmingly long broadsword she held in her right hand. Landing no more than six feet away, it was clear she dressed to impress and, fuck me, I was impressed big time!

'You expecting a barney luv?' I asked nervously.

As if in answer she held the tip of her sword to my throat and replied, 'I am always prepared Mr Crowley. Fair or foul, day or night, heaven or hell. One thousand years ago I was not prepared and was murdered by the Celtic King, Teudar the Great.'

'I don't think I would have thought he was 'Great' if he'd bumped me off darlin!' I quipped, 'Mind you I guess that's why you're a saint eh?' Couldn't fault her preparation these days mind, and I for one wouldn't have had a bet against her now as she was clearly dressed to kill. Literally.

The cigarette had fallen clumsily from my lips as she raised the sword, thankfully away from my gullet and pointed to a plaque on the church wall about seven feet up. This plaque presented a story which was a little difficult to decipher at that height and that time of night. I made out a figure being hanged from a gibbet and a date, so I got the gist nevertheless.

IA sat down on the bench, seemingly a little crestfallen and I re-seated myself respectfully at her side to listen to her tale.

'I wanted you here at this noiseless time Mr Crowley to tell you of the events of 1549 and also to explain how they will affect you personally now.'

Blimey, I love a bit of Jackanory but she imparted the whole X-rated tale about this knight of old, referred to thenceforth as the Provost Marshall, who had visited the town, enjoyed a celebratory nosh up with the local mayor in those days known as the Portreeve and as soon as he had pigged out, walked his generous host out to the Market Place and strung the poor bastard up in front of the local townsfolk. That was a bedtime story to keep the kids awake at night all night for sure.

I leant an elbow upon my knee and quizzically inquired, 'You paint a pretty picture darlin' but what's this all got to do with me?'

IA's eyes burned through me and she seemed illuminated in the darkness.

'The Provost Marshall and the Portreeve will meet again soon magician, and this time they intend to hang you, in proxy!'

'That's very decent of them, errrm, why me?' I wondered aloud.

Before she continued her tale the saint balanced her sword on its tip between us on the bench and it now resembled a cross, a very shiny, very sharp cross. Calmly she explained the details further. 'It seems your recent ill-gotten business acquaintance Mr Bucca Dhu has invited these lamented charismas and their feud from the past, back to the town anew. Apparently, he feels threatened by your presence.'

I knew it! I couldn't trust the demon. But I had thought our business together had gone well enough and that he had profited sufficiently, for him to tolerate my presence on his manor. Seems I was wrong. He was going to bring in a couple of restless spirits to do his dirty work and IA explained in addition, that he would use a couple of easily secured local geezers of dubious repute as body hosts. Then, these two spirits could possess the hosts and dish out the physical and terminal damage to me without delay. Well, two plus two doesn't always make four, especially when you have a saint on your side. Thank goodness for her warning. Why was she on my side?

I stood and stretched. I was trying not to look too alarmed, after all, it wouldn't be the first time someone had tried to kill me, would it? 'Well, it's time for bed' I yawned, 'can't tempt you, can I?' I continued cheekily, 'err.... no, I didn't think so! Why have you warned me IA?' The question hung gracelessly in the air.

Rising gently upwards, her wings fluttered lightly and silently, moving with angelic efficiency. 'Joint interest magician, I do not wish restless spirits to destabilise my town. The mortal protagonists are known to your friend Mr de Faux. I will text you their names. I bid you farewell for now.'

And with that she was gone.

'Yeah... Be lucky!' I cried after her, not of course expecting any further response.

On the way back to the studio, I took a little time to study the market place. My mind was racing with what had just been explained. Things were getting weirder by the minute. Not only had I somehow got a saint in tow, but this one even had a mobile phone and once I started up the Fore Street incline, her text arrived as promised. The first attached picture was a reminder of the story as its subject was the church wall plaque which retold her story of the Provost Marshall and the Portreeve. Nice of the town's first citizen to feed the hungry knight on his travels, although I bet he didn't expect the throttling at the end. Maybe he didn't eat his greens?

The next part of the text featured a couple of portraits of the two ancient adversaries. The Provost Marshall was Sir Anthony Kingston apparently. He looked a bit of a bruiser while the unsuspecting Mayor, His Honour John Payne, looked fairly typical of the medieval political elite. He certainly didn't look short of a bob or two that's for sure. The plaque's wording described in brief the events and the unfortunate conclusion of what appeared to be a religious dispute nearly five hundred years before. So these were the two restless spirits Bucca had summoned. Cheeky bugger! After all I did for him! The final part of the text displayed the two local scallies that Bucca had sourced, intended for the spirit hosts' occupation. Their unholy mission was to re-enact their feud, only this time it seemed that I was the intended lump of flesh that would dangle. The scallies were a native shopkeeper called Phillip Browne and a resident artist, Richard Soul, who both looked like a couple of tossers at first glance. I suppose they had to be if Bucca Dhu had them in his crosshairs.

The walk back to the studio must have taken much longer than necessary as I studied the local landscape in deeper detail. Homework and preparation would be key if I was to avoid my intended fate.

Once back at the apartment, I threw my jacket over the back of the armchair swearing to myself that that would be the only thing of mine hanging around here anytime soon.

Shortly afterwards I was lying on the bed smoking, and it wasn't only the cigarette that was smouldering, the old grey matter was burning with the one main realisation that I couldn't leave Bucca at large, following our coming skirmish. Of course, it had always been my intention to 'rope' him into the action from the minute the traitorous bastard had been sussed by IA. The sun was just coming up when I finally dozed off. My old man used to do nights and it made him a right grumpy git. I had considered asking Booby to knock up some curtains for this gaff as I never could sleep during the daytime. Should have been a bloody vampire, now there was a thought! Perhaps later?

Tuesday lunchtime, Booby and I were sitting looking out the window of a quayside café. The Boho style eatery was comically called Maggie T's, named after its owner who was a much lovelier woman than the 1980s despot we all suffered back in the day. While clearly she was both attractive with her cover-all fringe and Chanel No.5 fragrance, she wasn't currently on my erogenous radar.

The rain was belting down, and the boats bobbed frantically in the harbour. The few people who were around were scampering for cover and, looking at the packed tearoom, it was obvious that business could be good when the weather was foul.

The black cat, who had become my ever-present nuisance companion, even boorishly when I went for a slash, was balanced on the window ledge looking at the storm highly amused as a fat old lady struggled with her inverted umbrella.

Maggie coughed and sheepishly pointed at the signs on the back of the door which I could only just make out due to the copious amount of cigarette smoke I had belched out. One sign said 'No Smoking' and the one below said 'No Dogs'. She came over to collect our empty cups just as the cat jumped into the middle of our table and I cockily inquired, 'Cat got your tongue luv? If you've got anything to say, please do so.'

She looked embarrassed as all the punters had heard my assertive comments and they were cowering, expecting a ruck. 'Err, no, well, yes. It's just that if the Environmental come in, they'll have my licence.' Her voice was as sweet as she was.

Booby was at his pompous best as he joined in uninvited, 'She's right Ally, you're sooooooooo rude!'

'What are you talking about man?' I snapped. 'It's not a dog! Here, have a fag darlin.'

She took me by surprise because, looking resigned, she accepted my offer, popping it between her rosy reds before moving away and, laughing aloud said, 'I'll get you both a refill.' A few of the other customers were chuckling to themselves discreetly and by the time the chirpy waitress had returned with fresh cups, not only was she puffing away on a cancer stick but so too were most of her clientele. Even Booby had got off his high horse and was enjoying a drag.

He was the first to speak in this newly relaxed environment. 'Great news Ally! My novel's selling like hot cakes. I don't know why, it's so early in the season. Seems we will have to print another thousand copies.'

It was the least I could do for the silly old sod. He had washed my clothes, fed me plus was keeping me well entertained. I wasn't sure what I was going to do with all the books I had purchased though, which had been delivered to the studio early that morning. They were now rotting in the pilchard cellar beneath the apartment. If the storm kept up and the tide came in much more, I was considering releasing them into the Atlantic.

'That's brilliant my old son. Anyway, come down off the clouds for a bit, I am going to ask you for a little assistance.' Booby looked absorbed as I continued, 'Seems old Mr Bucca Dhu is planning to err, relocate me, and we can't be having that, can we?'

'I'll help any way I can Ally,' he replied smartly. 'I thought he looked a bit dodgy the first time I clapped eyes on him. Mind you, I'm afraid I am not much use in a catfight!'

I quickly reassured him, 'No, no, don't worry about that type of thing Boobs, I just need a little local intel. Looks like the rain's stopping mate. Let's go, I need you to introduce me to a couple of indigenous reprobates.'

With that, I dropped a tenner tip on the table, smiled at Maggie like we had just had intercourse out the back while her husband held my coat, and we were through the door onto the cobbles. All three of us.

Next stop was a small, fronted shop entrance at the beginning of Fore Street. It was a pretentious bazaar like the ones on Portobello Road, selling what looked to me like high priced tat. The sign above the door identified this gaff with ironic innocence as 'The Glory Hole'.

A long diagonal decal on the door proclaimed, 'Where the riches of ages are stowed, anything and everything a chap can unload.'

'The owner's a bit of an arse, Ally. His name is Phillip Browne, with two L's. Full of himself I am afraid,' sighed Booby.

'Full of shit more like my old mate, judging by his strap line,' I replied.

With that the shop's owner appeared on the steps. Late fifties, a scruffy peacock type of a geezer who clearly considered himself superior and, doubtless in his mind, everybody on the planet owed him a good living. A sort of unwanted, too tall, film extra vibe reverberated.

'We're not open yet. Another three minutes,' he proffered aloofly.

Not waiting for an invite I just barged past him into the shop. A few of the wall fittings and displays crashed to the floor as, caught off balance, he collided with some of his stock. 'Oiy!' he cried, traumatised by my lack of respect, 'you will have to pay for any breakages, you ruffian!'

'Don't be silly Philly,' I countered, 'you should be paying me for coming into this dump in the first place.'

Booby hunched his shoulders toward the disconcerted shopkeeper in a feeble and embarrassed attempt at apology, while I continued, as now I was facing him and had lit up. 'Got some tat in 'ere Phill... Ever sell any of it?'

Phillip looked like he was about to explode as he answered condescendingly and loudly, 'I will have you know my patrons are a little more refined than where I imagine one such as you originates from my man!'

That was cutting, but I had had a lot worse than that so I moved closer to him and placed my index finger on the end of his beak.

'You shouldn't have said that Phillip my boy. That is going to cost you. How much is that axe up there?' I said, angrily pointing toward the Gibson Explorer guitar hanging from the low ceiling. Phillip, greedily remembering his retail manners and seeing a sales opportunity replied, 'Two thousand and not a penny less!'

Soon as I had secured the deal, which undoubtedly left peacock Phill a little confused and bewildered thanks to my 'persuasive and suggestive talents', otherwise known as auto- suggestive hypnotism, Bobby and I were on our way to our next meeting. My friend was kindly carrying the deviously purchased guitar, handsomely complemented of course by its pristine brown carrying case, although he was clearly somewhat flabbergasted with the deal I had just negotiated. 'I can't believe he let you have that for just twenty pounds Ally!'

'No, it was a little more than I wanted to pay mate. But at least he threw the case in, hey?'

Making our way smartly through the rest of the premier shopping street of the town, we entered the Market Place adjacent to the parish church. As we passed the bookshop I afforded myself a little smile at the sign in the window proclaiming that Booby's novel, 'High on the Tide' was sold out. 'More stock later this week' they promised.

The market square appeared to be in the middle of a refurb and there were builders, plus their subsequent masses of scaffolding cluttering up what was at normally a very congested scene anyway. A private hire cab with the legend, 'Tops Taxis' on its side was motionless with its bumper pressed hard against a distraught holidaymaker's shiny new Mercedes. The shabby taxi driver was leaning out the driver's window and in his finest Cornish drawl, he shouted over to one of the builders. 'Oiy! When you boys gonna be finished with all this mess? Is 'ard enough tryin to get round this town at the best of times without all your frameworks an' boards boy!'

The builder smiled pleasantly and replied diplomatically although undoubtedly, he didn't give a toss.

'Keep yer hair on mate, it won't be long now. Couple a days and we'll take this gallows down hah, hah, hah!'

I think it was that crack that gave me my next great idea.

Booby was busy bodying himself nosily, taking in the scene, and clumsily stumbled into a bucket of cement that was hanging at head height awaiting a roofer's pull upward on a block and tackle. 'Oh Ally!' he cried, as some of the mortar deposited itself upon his boat race. 'Look, I've got builders muck on my face now!'

'Wouldn't be the first time, would it?' I cracked as we moved away giggling like a couple of schoolgirls.

The bucket continued swinging on the block and tackle as it made its way up the scaffold and before it was gathered in by the waiting labourer, my idea had crystallised fully. We carried onwards and five minutes later were in a small avenue off the beaten track. Now I had sussed out our first scallywag, I wanted to meet the second.

Opposite a small gallery Booby stopped and then placing the guitar case against a wall, he looked imploringly at me as I paused to light up a fresh smoke. The frontage was a shit-tip with old books, magazines and CDs scattered haphazardly on the steps leading up to the entrance, all in scruffy plastic boxes and in the filthy windows were amateurish drawings and photographs of nudes and seascapes priced for the Aga Khan.

'Oh Christ Ally! This fellow is not a nice man at all. His name is Richard. Richard Soul. Watch him, he is likely to throw a punch if you push him too far.' I appreciated the warning, but faint heart and all that malarkey came to mind.

'The only thing that needs a push round here Boobs, is a broom. What a dump!'

I hadn't seen the wild-haired gritty looking character sat fiddling with an old camera in a dilapidated deckchair behind me, but he spoke now. 'Maybe you would like me to clean up just for you then. I don't suppose you'll be buying 'owt will you?' he growled in an out of synch northern accent.

'Ah! Dick by name, dick by nature I assume?' I replied mockingly to the seated pretend Picasso-cum-David Bailey.

With that, he launched himself out of his collapsing seat and swung a haymaker my way. I swerved its impact and the heavily off-balance artist found himself heading for the lower steps without, unfortunately for him, the protection of a crash helmet.

A horrified Booby had his hands to his face peeking through his fingers in dread anticipation of the imminent impact. The noise of skull on step was truly sickening, yet it was better than that of a fist on my face for sure. This was the second assault upon my person since my St Ives arrival and up to this point, I hadn't even had to throw a punch to do the damage needed to win a bout. Richard lay face down on the steps in the gallery doorway groaning, and the few passers-by who had witnessed the event were clearly concerned for his wellbeing, though not concerned enough, it seemed, to rush to his assistance. Booby on the other hand was down on his knees in no time at all trying to help my stricken assailant. I bent over to have a butchers also, not at my attacker, rather at the box of CD's balancing on the lower step. Luckily for me he hadn't collided with it during his concrete head-butt.

'Cor Boobs!' I exclaimed excitedly at my audio find, ''The Scream' by Siouxsie and the Banshees mate. This is the version with Helter Skelter on it. I've been after this baby for years!'

Booby wasn't impressed with my discovery and callousness as he appealed, 'Oh gracious Ally! Do you think he'll be alright? He took a nasty fall there.'

Well, he was right, it was a nauseating tumble, yet I was sure Richard would get over it. 'Don't worry mate.

This record came out in 1978 which was probably the last time he washed his underpants.'

It was at the least insensitive of me, but I did have my reputation to consider in front of the now gathering audience. As I walked off back to the studio pocketing my new find, I issued some rather flippant instructions, 'Slip him a fiver Boobs and don't forget to bring the guitar back with you. I might have a strum along session later if you're lucky.'

IA was sat on the armrest of the leather chair as I entered the apartment. Her Doc Martens were shined to a blood red gloss, while her wings were resting at her sides, the backpack placed squarely on the dining table. Deadly sexy with the emphasis on dead.

'Good evening, ma'am. Let yourself in any time, why don't you. Where's your pet?' I queried.

She pointed firmly toward the Island, visible through the open window, and at the chapel perched upon its summit, then spoke in severe tones.

'He is on lookout duty, Mr Crowley. Our unholy guests will arrive soon. They will need to obtain safe haven and rest before they seek you out. We will know they are here, thanks to 'my pet' as you call him, before they take asylum.'

Sitting down opposite her, whilst lighting a cigarette and trying to look composed, I asked, 'Where will they be safe from you then?'

'They will always be safe from me magician until I can trap them within the walls of my parish church,' she continued, not blinking an eye. 'That is where you come in, Mr Crowley, you shall lure them towards what will be their final destiny.' Suddenly I remembered the granite font with its angelic carvings that I had recognised earlier as disguised soul prisons and straight away realised what she was intending.

Darkness was just falling when I rounded the corner with the now backpacked IA. She pointed up the slope toward the large building nestling between the cobbled cottages to the rear of the Sloop Inn. 'That place was known as The Mariners' Church. It lost its preaching licence at the end of the last war and has been home to the town's Society of Artists ever since. It was only ever Anglican, so it shall hold no fear for the spirits of the avenging Provost Marshall or Portreeve.'

She didn't need to tell me much more. I had been in this game long enough to know what was coming next. The spooks would rest here once they had made landfall and then, when they had recovered full strength, they intended to possess the host bodies of the grumpy shopkeeper and the arty-farty bad-tempered artist. Next step was to pay me a visit and ensure that the evil favour Mr Bucca Dhu had requested of them, i.e. kill me, was carried out post haste. Watching IA walk away into the darkness, it seemed that my part was to attract the ghouls inside her church and Abracadabra - the saint would do the voodoo.

We soon arrived at the front entrance of the parish church. The evening had turned pitch black by now and the faint streetlights illuminated the clutter of Market Square, now all the builders had gone home. This place was where the original hanging had taken place nearly five hundred years before, so I was guessing that attracting my foes here wouldn't be too big an ask. This was also the place where IA had been martyred a thousand years before that, so I guessed she was feeling well and truly at home as well!

There was no more to be done tonight, so off I went to get some shuteye. Calling Booby on his mobile, I asked him if he could do me a nightshift. A simple reconnaissance mission with a twist. Other strategies and tactics had, after all, required planning so as to spoil the imminent hanging party.

I was awake long before daybreak and as I lay there smoking, I felt pleased that my plot was at least clear in my mind. It was not, of course guaranteed to work. However, given the commitment and support I had received thus far, I was pretty sure it had every chance.

I didn't see the black cat jump in through the window, but he was there at the end of the bed, arching his spine as if playing with an imaginary ball of wool. Agitated and with fangs bared, he clearly had a message of alert for me. They had arrived! Jumping out of bed, I was dressed and out on the cobbles in a flash.

It was 7am as I joined Booby who was sipping a mug of coffee outside on one of the Sloop Inn's bench seats. Bless him, he had got me a cuppa in too, so sitting tightly next to him, it was time to discover what he had witnessed during the night following my request.

'Flip me Ally. It's been a long night. I need my beauty sleep you know,' he said with a gaping yawn.

'Stop yer whingeing Boobs and tell me what you saw,' I countered rudely.

He didn't deserve that, he must have been frightened witless at what he had observed, so I tried to smooth things over, 'Sorry mate. You know I appreciate everything you are doing for me, don't you?'

'I know you do,' he blubbed, 'I'm not going to get hurt, am I Ally?'

Looking him squarely in the eye, I replied, 'Not if you do exactly what I say mate. Now tell me. What's occurred?'

Booby gave me a running commentary using some footage he had sneakily shot on his phone camera through a window of the Mariners' Church while balancing comically on a ladder he had 'borrowed' from the Market Place. Probably the only erection he had put up for years! On his small smartphone screen I could make out two ghostlike figures dressed in sixteenth century attire. One was an officious looking character decorated with chains of authority and the other one looked your typical period piece bloodthirsty adventurer. I couldn't help but look on unamused at the rope, complete with noose, this swashbuckler held at hip level. So, it seemed the ancient spirits of John Payne and Sir Anthony Kingston had indeed risen again at Bucca's command, as accurately described by IA. Tonight would be the night of their attack, once they had refreshed, revitalised and possessed their twenty-first century physical hosts.

Briefing Booby over another coffee as the populace began to emerge from the holiday apartments and businesses in preparation for what looked as if it was going to be another warm early summertime day, our own preliminaries were agreed, and we parted.

On my instructions, two hours later Booby was sat opposite Bucca Dhu in his darkened office. It couldn't have been a comfortable experience for him as he started to explain why he had requested this meeting on my behalf. 'Thanks for seeing me, Mr Dhu. Ally, errrm, Mr Crowley has asked me to invite you out for drinks tonight at eight'ish. He wants to celebrate your recent partnership and success at the card table.'

'Does he really Mr de Faux? I wondered when he would get around to sharing the spoils,' said the cloaked demon sardonically.

Booby continued as I had instructed him, 'Oh yes, he has your share of the winnings all ready for you neatly packaged, plus a rather special gift I am sure you will cherish.'

Bucca's face was framed in query, the hand placed under his chin emphasising his long, pointed fingernails. 'Special, cherish, Mr de Faux? I am intrigued. Eight o'clock it shall be then. Where shall we meet?'

'A neutral venue of your choice Mr Dhu. Mr Crowley was quite insistent that you picked it so you could be assured of your security' Booby continued, 'Somewhere this end of Fore Street would be good though.'

Bucca Dhu probably sensed some sort of subterfuge, but would feel more confident if he could pick the venue. 'The Castle Inn at 8pm then Mr de Faux. That will do nicely,' and with that he was on his feet showing Booby the exit with a contempt that was obvious to me in retrospect as Booby explained this all to me later on.

I loitered in a neighbouring doorway to make sure my accomplice was safe, watching him take his short staccato steps away from The Bizz like a naughty schoolboy. Once out into the sunlight and onto the Market Square, Booby hailed a Tops Taxicab in what was his effeminate and naturally offhand way, 'I would like to go to Penzance, my man. Could you oblige?'

'I'll oblige for twenty-five quid, alrighty boy!' came the salty reply. With that agreed and Booby on board, the taxi departed up the hill on its way out of the town. 'Where you want me to drop you luvey? The Pink Slipper, hah, hah, hah!'

'Cheeky devil!' bit Booby, 'that's for girls anyway! Now take me to Simpsons in the Penzance Market Place. They are stockists of the finest Aquascutum don't you know?'

'Whatever,' came the confused reply. The taxi disappeared into the distance, and it was more than a little amusing to notice that a seagull in salute, had deposited what was presumably a mixture of Cornish pasties and ice cream through its arsehole onto the rear window of the taxicab obscuring Booby's pompous physique.

Wednesday evening and Booby and I were already seated at a table just inside the door of the Castle Inn when Bucca Dhu entered smiling with his two henchmen, Flotsam and Jetsam. We didn't so much as notice the Rottweilers as smell them and although The Castle was known as a 'Dog Friendly' environment, there was nothing friendly about these two mutts.

The tabletop was decorated with my lager, Booby's G&T and a Guinness for our guest. Looking at the Irish draught Bucca Dhu seemed pleased. 'Ah, Mr Crowley, the black stuff! How did you know?'

I feigned surprise, 'Bleeding obvious mate!'

The demon seated himself with his back to the door, making sure his minders had the exit well covered as he took a sip of his pint.

'Our business the other night was a great success my friend. St Ives is better off without Contattio and his sort.'

'Yes,' I agreed, 'Much better off with you and your sort I would imagine.'

'Exactly!' the demon proclaimed, amused.

Placing a black leather briefcase on the table, in my peripheral vision I noticed the other drinkers moving gently outwards, away from where we were seated, obviously expecting a hubbub of some sort. Booby stayed resolute, his trust in me was gratifying as I cut to the chase. 'Your share Mr Dhu. It was nice to see that you trusted me not to leg it with the lot the other night.'

'No, no, no, I never thought that for a minute Mr Crowley. Of course, I trusted you my friend,' he returned.

That was nice of the two-faced bastard, that's why he had invited the killer knight and the old-style murdered mayor over then was it?

Bucca Dhu opened the case top just enough to take a peek at the neatly stacked cash inside which was slightly north of 175K. While he was salivating Booby took the opportunity to place two large shopping bags on the empty chair beside him. The bag's logo was classy and stated, 'Simpsons – The Finest Gentlemen's Outfitters since 1860'.

Bucca looked titillated. 'Ah, Mr de Faux, you said your friend had bought me a special gift, one that I would cherish and looking at the label I am thinking you will be most correct.'

I innocently re-joined the conversation, 'I got one for each of us in celebration of our partnership. Thought it might bring a little class to the proceedings and give us something to remember the occasion by, if nothing else.' We opened our wrappings together and the cloaked monster looked as pleased as the proverbial when he realised that we now had matching trench coats and not just normal ones, the very top of the range models.

'Mr Crowley! I am honoured and indeed will treasure your gift, although we must not show off when we parade,' he said, chuckling to himself.

'My pleasure guv, it was nice doing business with you. Let's hope we can do so again soon.'

While we exchanged pleasantries, at the other end of Fore Street, Phillip Browne was locking up his shop for the night and I am sure he didn't feel a thing as the misty spirit figure of Sir Anthony Kingston, complete with rope and noose entered his body taking instant control of his every move and thought. Simultaneously, at the gallery off the beaten track, the badly bruised proprietor, Richard Soul exited his premises to be instantly and completely possessed by the ghostly Portreeve's spirit. Both these respected, yet unlikable characters had then commenced their zombie-like journeys at a reckless pace, heading our way directly, which opportunely, was at the conclusion of our little drink with the traitorous Mr Bucca Dhu.

Our drinking party was now standing just outside the Castle Inn amongst an interested but transient audience, admiring the pristine trench coats. 'Thank you again, Mr Crowley, the fit is perfect, I could not be more delighted!' explained the excited demon as Booby chipped in with his own perfectly timed plaudits, 'Oh! You look so handsome Mr Dhu. You and Ally look like twins, I must say.' Of course, that was my intention, but the comparison thankfully was lost on the fiend as he was still too busy admiring his gift to pay much attention to the compliment. 'Errrm, thank you, Mr de Faux,' he said half-heartedly.

Our motley group walked off together towards the Market Place. Bucca and I were at the head smoking a couple of the demon's best cigars. Flotsam, Jetsam and the two dogs were only a few paces behind, and Booby had remembered my instructions and left an appropriate gap, faking a loose bootlace as a delaying tactic. From behind, Bucca and I did indeed look like two peas in a pod. Unbeknown to him, a simple cloaking spell I had enacted earlier would make me look more like his shadow than his associate.

We walked, chatting pleasantly together and, other than the fact that Bucca carried the loot-filled briefcase we looked identical. I had indicated we would part company just before the church, explaining that Booby and I would like to walk back along the quay road so we could enjoy the harbour view before we turned in. He and his bodyguards would turn right and return to The Bizz no doubt, looking forward to my extermination at the hands of his supernatural servants.

I had made sure Bucca was walking on the inside of the street, so as to be backlit by the retailers' lights whilst I was hugging the kerb engulfed in the darkness. That way, I could ensure he looked every bit the star of the evening's entertainment and our silhouettes were in stark contrast as we entered the Market Place area.

The crazed figures of Phillip Browne and Richard Soul came into view. Both were running at a full tilt, convening on the oblivious Bucca Dhu. Phillip was energetically spinning his rope and noose around his head like a cowboy about to cut out a rogue steer from the herd. With a scream that alerted all and sundry to the pair's presence, Phillip launched himself like a crazed harpy, landing with a sickening thud in the middle of Bucca Dhu's back. Now that the demon had had the wind knocked out of his sails along with the briefcase from his hand, Phillip slipped the noose around his neck, all in one swift efficient motion.

Never one to look a gift horse in the mouth, I collected the briefcase from the side of the road and instantly observed the demented spirit of Richard Soul gathering up the end of the rope that had been passed him by his supernatural accomplice. Before Bucca had a chance to gather his wits or his breath, Richard had thrown the rope end over the building scaffold's lowest hanging horizontal pole and as the rope end fell back down to earth, both of the unearthly assassins were ready to catch it. A number of innocent bystanders along with Booby, Flotsam and Jetsam looked on in horror whilst the two Rottweilers took off like shit from a shovel with their discarded leads flapping behind them like ribbons. I began to sprint for the parish church's front entrance. With a mighty yank, Phillip and Richard hauled the stricken demon off the pavement and into the air by his neck and there was an almighty crack as his neck was snapped.

By this time, I was standing in the church doorway, cheerfully observing this extreme case of mistaken identity, though realising that it wouldn't be too long before the gruesome twosome realised their disastrous blunder and attempted to put it right, no doubt at my expense!

I yelled to Booby and by default the two idiot henchmen, who were standing dumbstruck, 'Run! They'll soon realise they got the wrong guy!' All three of them took off and I was happily surprised to see Booby winning the race toward the open doorway where I stood backing further inward, issuing the instructions, 'Quick! Inside now!' All three runners entered the church doorway together and the inevitable collision of their panicked bodies brought them crashing headlong into the lobby area. The two chasing hardly human ghouls didn't wait on ceremony, hurdling the stricken trio as if they were on their way to Olympic Gold. It wasn't ceremonial hardware they were after though, it was more, not to put too fine a point on it, my arse!

Richard had retrieved his rope from the now deceased demon's neck and this time he sent it lasso style in my direction. These guys couldn't have known how good I was at ducking and diving and in fact, turning defence into attack so, avoiding the lariat, I grabbed the noose end in my right hand and, pulling violently, managed to wrench both Richard and the handily collected Phillip toward me. 'C'mere you Bastards!' I cried as they fell face first, and compromisingly stricken at my feet. I now stood adjacent to the church font and although the rest of the religious furniture was traditionally drab, the large stained glass window of Saint EIA behind me glowed magically iridescent. I noticed all four of the granite angels cast on the body of the font and knew two of them were shortly to be utilised as the camouflaged soul prisons I'd noticed on my first visit to the church.

Directly behind me stood IA in her full battle dress, armed to the teeth and with her wings spread. Without formality I addressed the two recovering spirit husks of Phillip and Richard, now kneeling before me as if in repentance.

'Gentlemen! Let me introduce you to your, err, nemesis!'

With that IA unleashed hellfire from her broadsword and the entire church was backlit with a blinding flash. The whole atmosphere was charged with electrical force and it took ten seconds for the ether to settle. Richard and Phillip were gone. I noticed straightaway that two of the angel's images on the font were smouldering and the engraved likenesses had changed perceptibly to that of the St Ives shopkeeper and the artist.

Reaching inside my coat pocket I coolly retrieved my cigarettes. Booby and the now unemployed henchmen looked relieved. Leading the shell-shocked clique out of the church, I found myself mumbling under my breath to the vanished IA, 'See you around sometime darlin', not too soon I hope!'

It had been a hell of a night for all of us and as I passed beholding again the granite font and its new tenants, a humble thought crossed my mind - I had, indeed, 'killed two birds with one stone,' so to speak and a good time had been had by well, very nearly all!

Part Three

A Darker Monarch

Sitting on the harbour wall outside Maggie T's café and reading the paper with a cup of tea balancing dangerously on the undulating hard grey granite surface, I was in a happy holiday mood. I was seasonally dressed in my blue shorts, white T-shirt and red flip flops, all topped off dashingly with the darkest pair of shades you could ever imagine. Saturday morning had arrived uneventfully and thankfully things had quietened down in the town following the recent pandemonium.

The local rag was called the St Ives Times and Echo and was broadsheet in size. I was engrossed with the local art scene reviews. Any by-passer though, would have read the front cover's sensational headlines. In bold font the headers proclaimed, 'Local Businessman Murdered in the Market Square'. A smaller title caption read 'Police called to pub riot' with a picture of the smashed-up Bizz. Pleasantly in contrast the back page had a large image of a handful of surfers with the legend 'UK Surfing Championships this Weekend at Porthmeor Beach'. Well, it wasn't all bad news then!

Underneath the lower skirt of the paper a couple of pairs of black size tens appeared and without looking, I sensed the presence of the local porksters. Peering over the rim of the periodical I welcomed my visitors with the routine, 'Hello, hello, hello, what have we got 'ere then!'

The two men were stereotypical plain clothes, both black suited, they obviously shopped unimaginatively at Marks and Spencers. The older man, who appeared to be about fifty, had a shaven head and held out his warrant card as if he was expecting me to let him into Wembley Stadium on the strength of it. 'Very funny Mr, errrm, Crowley, isn't it?'

'Well, I don't suppose that's really a guess, is it El Capitan?' I replied discourteously.

The second man who was blond and about thirty moved in close, trying to intimidate me as he yelled and glared, 'Show some respect you tosser or we'll have you down the nick so fast you'll get a nosebleed!'

There was an unpleasant delay, then the more senior policeman apologised for his colleague's over-aggressive introduction, 'Please forgive Sgt Watts's manner Mr Crowley, he is a trifle forceful on occasion.

His army training, I don't doubt. I am Inspector Armstrong, and I was hoping we could have a little chat?'

I couldn't help laughing as I started to reply, but I quickly turned malevolent. 'Tell your arse-wipe to wind his neck in Inspector, otherwise I will have to introduce him to civilian life, starting with the ambulance service!'

The sergeant moved in closer still, but the inspector verbally restrained him, 'Not now Watts, this is not the time or place.'

With my little finger outrageously extended toward the pissed-off plod, I took a large sip of my fast-cooling drink and continued, 'Hear, hear Inspector. Tell your mate to fuck off will you? He's curdling the milk in my cuppa.'

The angry Sgt Watts departed following his guvnor's less offensive instruction, making his way to the café as the inspector started over again, 'That was a little cruel Mr Crowley. He doesn't appreciate being spoken to like that.'

'No, I don't suppose a bully like that ever does, Inspector,' I replied offhandedly.

The policeman leaned against the wall trying to look informal with his hands in his trouser pockets.

'Things have been a little lively around here the last few days Mr Crowley. How long have you been in town exactly?'

I mocked up my best quizzical look and remaining seated, uttered my request, 'Cut to the chase Clouseau. What do you want?'

It was the usual story. He knew I was behind the disturbances, just couldn't prove it. Even if he could have done so, he probably wouldn't have bothered, seeing as I had just lightened his workload by removing the majority of his worst nuisance neighbours, all in one go.

Turning away from me, he motioned with a hand no longer playing pocket billiards and said, 'Try to enjoy your holiday Mr Crowley, delight in the sunshine and the sea. The weather, they say, is set fair. Give me a chance to catch up with all the paperwork at least, hey?'

With that remark unanswered, he re-joined his colleague outside the café, collecting his own takeaway coffee in passing from the still glaring Sgt Watts. I waved them both a sarcastic goodbye and even at that distance I could see the veins bulging in the sergeant's neck. He was right mind I did come here for a bit of R & R and so far it had been more like a Carry On film. I resolved to take the inspector's advice and chill.

I don't know what I looked like in the hired wetsuit, but Booby resembled a miniature whale in a condom! Booking the surfing session that morning, I couldn't have appreciated that a couple of hours later, my newfound friend and I would be the only adults in the lesson group. It was mostly young kids aged six to fifteen and we must have looked a right sight, self-consciously milling around the large learner boards laid out on the sand awaiting the young, fit and bronzed surf instructors.

'I don't know why I agreed to this Ally! Just look at me!' protested Booby, only I couldn't help laugh wickedly in his face. Soon our party was joined by our instructors and in a thick Australian accent the cockier one of the pair introduced himself.

'Gooday everybody! I'm Bruce and this is Sime,' he said, indicating his mate at his side. 'We're going to help you guys master the waves today. Firstly though, I'd like you to stick one of these super-duper yellow T-shirts on.' There was nothing super or duper about them, as once they were fitted snugly on top of our wetsuits, we looked like mobile advertising boards for the St Ives Surfing Club.

'That's great guys and girls, you all look fab! Are you all ready to have a great time?' Bruce emphasised his last few words heavily and the kindergarten surfers responded in unison with an excited, 'Yeaaaaaaaaaaah!'

With that, the group embarked on a few gentle prescriptive exercises designed to loosen our limbs and stretch our muscles before we entered the water. Booby was puffing and panting as we trotted along the beach. I bet he was picked last for every school team. I kept up as best I could with the teenage tearaways out in front, just to let them know that I wasn't as far over the hill as they had all imagined. Once we had warmed up we all headed down to the shoreline with our big, yellow and blue soft boards. Having been paired off unsuitably with someone of similar 'vibes' as Bruce put it, we carried the boards two at a time, one person holding the front noses under each arm while the other partner mirrored the rear ends. Apparently, this was the norm, designed to counteract any cross winds and my partner was a tall, gangly youth of about fifteen, while Booby trailed behind a ten-year-old Bonnie Langford lookalike, pigtails, and all. The whole scene must have looked particularly comical, if not a little worrying for any onlookers, especially, I imagined, the children's parents.

We all sat in a semicircle just short of the tide mark as Sime took over the instructions, 'Right team, we're nearly ready to hit the water only first I need to explain a few of the basics.'

'Cheer's Sime!' Bruce clearly thought he was the boss and took back over from his less forthright, but now piqued partner, before he could establish any rapport. 'Only three instructions you need to remember out there, let's have a quiz,' he commanded, and then pointing across his chest with his right arm pointing left, he said, 'What do you reckon this means mates?' A young chubby faced tyke at the front of the group who was clearly destined to become the teacher's pet answered cockily, 'Go left!' Bruce looked at the kid with murder in his eyes as the brat had obviously spoilt his big reveal and he responded unkindly, 'Been surfing before have you sonny? What's your name?'

'My name's Timmy and yes, I have surfed before mister, many times and I am rather good at it,' replied the obnoxious, yet extremely entertaining, little brat.

'Ok, so what does this mean, then?' Bruce held his left arm across his chest pointing right this time and added, 'not you Timmy,' before the little toe rag could spoil his fun. There was silence as none of the other kids dared to speak. Booby though couldn't help himself, 'That must mean go right then?' He offered helpfully. Bruce focussed on Booby's sweet round face and without any irony confirmed his answer as, 'Correct!'

Next, he pointed upwards into the sky with his right arm and blew his whistle hard, 'Anybody other than Timmy and that guy know what that means then?'

'Low flying seagull?' I called out harmlessly and a few of the kiddiewinks nodded, thinking that I might be right. 'Not a bad try chum,' said Bruce, totally oblivious to the fact that I was taking the piss. 'In fact,' he concluded, 'it means get out now.' That must have made him feel very important I presumed. So, only three instructions and no offside then, definitely my type of sport I thought.

Sime took the opportunity to take back command while his self-important partner enjoyed his status in smug contemplation and explained, 'There's also only three things to worry about out there in the water guys. The tide, the rocks, and most importantly other surfers.' So needing a piss wasn't one of the worries then? 'If you pay those things attention and respect you can't go wrong boys and girls and errrm, you two,' he said, belatedly.

Booby raised his arm concerned-pupil-like, and with an anxious look on his face posed the question that all the others were afraid to ask, for fear of looking stupid, 'What about the sharks?'

'Don't worry buddy,' replied the officious Australian. 'There aren't any to worry about around this neck of the woods. Water's too bloody cold, hah, hah, hah!' Then he turned his head to the side, and I caught him whispering cruelly to his opo, 'Fuckin' spit him out if they had a bite anyway!' And with that, we were off to the water's edge.

Bruce and Sime marched into the surf cheerfully and their infectious gusto was rubbing off a treat for all involved, excepting Booby who looked a little apprehensive as the not inconsiderable waves washed around his meat and two veg. A little gee up was obviously required from yours truly. 'Come on son! Crack that face and give it a bash will yer!' And with that advice, a larger wave knocked him off his feet and under the water completely. It was a salty baptism and once he had regained his footing, he looked resigned to his fate, well at least the next hour or so anyway.

The tide came back in a bit quicker than we did as it turns out, because against the odds, we all had a bloody good laugh. I managed proudly to get upright a couple of times whilst Booby succeeded in recycling a couple of gallons of seawater through his lungs and out of his nose! Leaving the boards on the shore ready for the next lesson, I thanked our instructors while Booby broadcast to all and sundry that he needed a stiff drink to get over his ordeal. 'Come off it old son, we had a whale of a time. That was the most fun either of us has had for years!' I claimed, to which his smiling face was more than enough confirmation.

Ominously, there was large dark shadow lurking less than twenty metres away in the shallows and in my mellow mood I naively thought of seaweed. Trudging back up the beach, tired but elated following our escapades, it's safe to say that in retrospect, if anything sinister did momentarily break the surface, we along with everybody else on the seashore missed it. Once my fatigued companion and I had athletically liberated ourselves from the rented wetsuits, we walked back up the ramp that transferred us out onto the road to the front of the Tate Gallery. At least, I thought contentedly, I couldn't get myself or anybody else into trouble while I was having such a surprisingly good time. What had IA said? That's right, 'a magnet for ne'er do wells – both human and other.' Well, she had been right about that, but not today. I put down my mental marker forcefully. No ne'er do wells, no humans and certainly no others causing me grief at the moment. How wrong could I have been!

Back at the studio apartment we were doing what the British do best, drinking tea and smoking cigarettes whilst looking out through the large French doors at the magnificent view. Booby croaked out a feeble, 'Oheerr! I feel all bruised and battered inside Ally. I don't think I got the hang of that 'Pop-up' lark did I?' he queried, trying to court sympathy.

None was forthcoming however, as I quipped back, 'No mate! It did look more like a 'Pop-out' from where I was standing, ha, ha, ha!'

Booby smiled painfully, albeit graciously, and continued, 'Well, at least you were right. It was jolly good fun.'

'Yeah, it was fab Boobs. I did find myself at peace for once, I must admit,' and having said that, within five minutes both of us were sound asleep, snoring loudly I would imagine, while the afternoon sun outside began to cool as it disappeared under the horizon.

Darkness had fallen when I awoke and as my consciousness returned gently, through gummy eyelids I saw a large seagull perched on the guard rail banister. Not one to be surprised by much these days, I must admit I was taken aback when the bird opened its beak and began to talk, 'Mr Crowley. Wake up!'

I wondered if this was all an unfortunate extension of the pleasant dream I was having but the bird spoke again, 'It's not a dream Mr Crowley. Suspend your disbelief and listen to me with an open mind, I beseech you.'

Not moving from my armchair and having confirmed that Booby was still asleep, totally unaware of this strange scene, I countered, 'Don't suppose I should be too surprised, should I? Who the fuck are you?'

Turning sideways on, the bird presented himself as the great raconteur and commenced with his biography.

'Ah, I am glad you have asked. I am Sven. Once of this blot on the landscape. A great poet and artist who was cruelly abused by my enemies, my peers and even my heroes. When I died, I was refused a pass over due to a saintly misunderstanding and I am instead confined within the boundary of this town and doomed forever to shit on those and theirs, who shat on me in life.'

It was a heart-breaking tale, one though that had enough comedic appeal for me to make the acidic observation, 'I bet you're a bastard when you see an unprotected pasty as well huh?'

Ashamedly he replied, 'Bit of a devil with an ice cream I am afraid to say as well, Mr Crowley. Given the chance, of course!' It would all have been hilarious if it hadn't had been so surreal.

'Now I know who you are, I guess it's only fair to ask, what do you want?'

The seagull shifted his weight and turned to face me.

In all solemnity he continued, 'It's not so much what I want, it is much more complex than that. I, along with many other animals it seems, find myself strangely attracted to your existence upon the Penwith Peninsula. Your presence brings great numbers of us here to worship you, and also brings out the worst of our natural behaviour. It's not just the indigenous species either Mr Crowley, those breeds not ordinarily seen here and about are visiting with malevolent hearts and thoughts.'

Lighting a cigarette I thought I summed his tale up quite well. 'What like flies to shit you mean?'

'So to speak,' he confirmed. Then turning outwards he sprang from the bannister leaving me a warning as he swooped away into the night, 'No good can come of this. Many will suffer. You need to take responsibility before these beasts create mayhem!'

Fucking hell! It wasn't unusual for the Law to feel my collar but I supposed it was a bit rich for a gut on legs to tell me to get a grip. The flutter of wings caused Booby to stir and he stretched his arms, looking uncomfortably cramped whilst trying to work out which of his limbs had died in his sleep.

'Oh Ally, what a strange dream I was having. Have I missed anything?'

'No, no, mate just a talking seagull is all!' I responded, to which Booby grimaced, interpreting the comments as childish and satirical.

Booby was a dab hand with the frying pan and while I was stuck in my thoughts, he was whipping up a tasty evening supper, chattering away as he proceeded.

'You are a wag Ally! Talking seagulls indeed! Flying rats, my old mum used to call them. Never mind, I'll make us a nice Spanish omelette.'

He was happy in his work, quite the little housewife, nonetheless my mind was racing because I knew instinctively that I should take the seagull's advice seriously. Feeling that only half the story had been shared so far, I resolved to do some research. Why would the wildlife have a hard on for me anyway? It's one thing having a local mutt shag your leg, but I was sure Sven meant a whole lot worse than that was coming. Although lost deep in my considerations, I was brought back to earth as Booby positioned the dinner plate on the table where I had been sitting drumming my fingers. It looked very appetising.

'Blimey Boobs, this all looks hale and hearty mate.'

With his smug face on he replied, 'You know what they say, you only get out what you put in.'

'You must have eaten a lot of sausage then,' I jested. Both of us could do no more than snicker throughout our meal, as our friendship had developed into something genuine since being thrown together by circumstance.

First thing in the morning, well eleven o'clock is normally first thing for me anyway, I was half way up Treggana Hill. Once past the specialist boutique shops and the galleries, the pet shop was easily identifiable by its rather colourful window display of dog leads and collars. This was as good a place as any to start my enquiries, as I had noticed on my passing the other night after my pow wow with the saint, the unique, yet subtle alchemical and protection symbols, either carved or drawn into the shop's wooden frontage borders.

Entering the small empty shop, a warning bell was triggered at the top of the door frame and the high pitched 'Ding a Ling a Ling' sounded quaint but in keeping with the jumbled, above suspicion looking environment. Initially I didn't see the bespectacled old man seated behind the counter with his long white hair and beard, as he was chameleon-like amongst the surroundings, however, my sense of smell was certainly assaulted since the room stank like something nasty had recently taken a dump.

The old man looked up above the rims of his spectacles and addressed me coldly and directly, 'Yes young man, is it a cat issue?'

'There's always a cat issue in this town chief,' I responded as the old man eyed me up as a potential adversary.

He removed his glasses completely as he stood, seemingly satisfied that I posed no instant threat, and continued his assessment.

'I saw you the other night with the cat following you. He is known to me as 'The Black Manilishi' and I assumed he was in need?'

'Oh, he's in need, all right, squire, of my boot right up his arse,' I teased.

The old man shuffled from behind his counter toward me. He was stooped and ancient beyond earthly years. Once past me, he eagerly flipped the door sign over to 'Closed' and pulled the blind down to make sure we would not be disturbed. 'Follow me into the backroom young man,' he instructed, 'I am sure you could learn to love him. I have known him for nearly two hundred years and I have come to appreciate his errrm, charms.'

'I noticed your charms old man, all over your woodwork. I see them for the protection symbols that they are. What are you afraid of?'

He led me through the doorway between the shop and his living accommodation and answered, 'I step to the dark side only rarely these days, though I always like to be prepared. I believe you have already met a few of the local supernaturals, Mr Crowley?'

It seemed like every man, dog, cat, saint and seagull knew who I was already, but it wasn't long before I found myself trusting this stranger absolutely. His parlour looked like a traditional but untidy Victorian sitting room. There were mystic appliances and paraphernalia scattered all around and I was pleased with his unconventional offer of refreshments. 'I don't do tea and coffee Mr Crowley,' and with that, he poured two large drinks from an old half empty rum bottle and sat melancholy on his fireplace hearth. The room also held a birdcage, complete with a parrot who was not a prisoner, as the cage door was wide open. There was also I totalled, half a dozen dogs, more cats, a monkey and a few tropical birds flitting around the room.

'Are you Doctor Dolittle by any chance?' I asked, unwisely bolting the first drink down as it burnt my throat.

'Good God, no! He wasn't real!' was the tongue-in-cheek reply, 'whereas I am very much genuine Mr Crowley. I was baptised Peter. Peter Green. I am known around these parts as the, 'Friendly Old Pet Shop Boy' or 'Pet Shop Pete'. He necked his own thirst-quencher and gasped, 'Arrh, I always liked the rum, goes back to my fishing days when I needed the warmth.'

Peter offered me a seat on one of his two beaten-up fireside chairs and as soon as I was seated, all the animals crowded around me, looking to me as if I was the Messiah. I found it all a tad startling at the time. The parrot sat on my shoulder like a scene out of 'Treasure Island' while the monkey jumped up onto the chair's armrest and promptly downed a bottle of cider that he had collected on the way. The rest of the cats and dogs laid around my feet, except one a small Yorkshire Terrier who promptly jumped up on my lap and proceeded, unhelpfully, to wet herself. My now also seated host observed these actions with some trepidation and began, 'You see, my friend they are in awe of your presence and young Saffire there is more than a little fearful as well as a little damp!'

I removed the dripping hound from my lap sympathetically.

'Looks like she's just wet the baby's head! Why is she so afraid of me anyway?'

Peter shrugged his shoulders as if his answer was obvious.

'The same reason we fear the Lord. Power! You have the power and they recognise it. They are yours to command, but if you do not do so, they will assume you wish them to terminate those others who do not honour you.'

'So for some reason they hold me in high regard?'

'Yes, the reasons are clear Mr Crowley. You have done commerce with a saint and destroyed a demon, plus there is another's attendance amongst our little scene and he will amplify your charms for his own aims, given the opportunity.'

With that last statement the old man held up a book, open on its first page. A picture of a portly yet brutally handsome man wearing a leather captain's hat was prominent. He had a beard and looked like he would have been good in a scrap.

Peter continued, 'This is he to whom I refer. I believe you have already met him in his winged seabird identity. Sven Berlin, The Dark Monarch himself!'

Peter turned the 'Closed' sign back to 'Open' the minute I departed his shop. Although I was strangely charmed by his presence in the town, I pondered on this benevolent old wizard posing as a pet shop proprietor.

Further down the hill I turned right onto the High Street and soon I stood lighting up and gazing into the large window frontage of St Ives Holiday Breaks. The town's retailers seemed to love a sandwich board and there was another one blocking the pavement, obstructing a couple of pissed off home-grown and embarrassingly overgrown skateboarders, who clearly wanted to demolish it, as it was hindering their dangerous, small-wheeled pastimes and show-off stunts. 'UK Surf Champs at Porthmeor today 1.30pm' the board proclaimed. Well, I had an hour or so to get there and in jest I wanted to see if any of them could do better than me and Boobs.

So what did I know so far? The Dark Monarch who had already semi-introduced himself to me, kitted out as a seagull on my window guard rail! Peter had explained in some detail that although Sven had 'died' fifteen winters previous, his spirit had been trapped here by IA who had commanded him to look after the interests of the native wildlife as some sort of punishment for his previous beastly behaviour. It seemed that over the years his powers had evolved beyond her control and now he was so incensed and desperate because of his incarceration, he was on a do or die quest for his spiritual freedom. He had spotted an opportunity to hand over his unwanted responsibilities to yours truly and then intended to split the scene pronto. I would then be left to control his pack on my tod. It wasn't a gig I fancied but the cunning fucker had found a way to put me under pressure by making sure all the animals for miles around would seek me out and worship me as their new master, causing chaos as they went. It wasn't only the indigenous species either that he had summoned, as I was soon, alarmingly, to find out. All these poor creatures thought they were doing my will, deeming any that didn't bow down to me were the enemy and should be destroyed. What a rotter! What a dilemma! What was I going to do? Well, go and watch the surfing for a start.

Fore Street was packed with competition spectators making their way to the beach. There was also now a huge orange sticker across the bookshop window pronouncing, 'High on the Tide, second printing completely sold out. New stock next Wednesday – Reserve your signed copy now'. Christ!

By the time I was passing The Glory Hole at the other end of the street, I had condensed my thoughts down into one simple fact. Sven had been trapped here for fifteen years and it appeared that if he could kick up enough bad Karma, he could pass his burden on to me. Considering the way the animals had reacted in the pet shop, it seemed like he was halfway there. St Ives is great for a holiday, but I wasn't intending to spend an eternity here in command of an animal empire I never wanted in the first place. The sign in the Glory Hole's front widow read: 'Closed for business – owner away'. This reminded me of last week's events. I wondered how many more restless spirits and supernatural practitioners there were floating around the vicinity. Regardless of how many though, they all seemed to want a piece of my arse!

Anyway, surf's up!

Porthmeor beach was brim-full with the beautiful people and the Red Bull stands and pagodas accentuated the premier sporting event that was about to kick off. The waves were helpfully big, so Booby and I sat down on the sands with a clear view of the action, complete with wicker picnic hamper and binoculars.

'Oh! He's a big boy! He, he, he!' said Booby, looking through a pair of rather expensive field glasses

I suspected he had borrowed from our absent landlord. The glasses were pointed towards a handsome young man in white swim trunks, and I gathered he wasn't speaking about the geezer's height. Out on the waves a number of contestants were warming up practising their tricks and turns and jealously I observed a number of young girls on the beach presumably cheering on their boyfriends. A deep klaxon master-blaster air-horn sounded and the competition was in play.

'Well Boobs, I'm going to enjoy this,' I enthused. 'Nice weather, my kind of sport and more than a few other pretty attractions to keep me entertained. What could possibly go wrong today?'

Another stupid question, but how was I to know? Not really understanding the rules it was easier to just enjoy the thrills and spills in the afternoon sun and everything continued pleasantly enough, right up until the senior event commenced.

An excited Booby, now glued permanently to his binoculars, pointed out to the waves.

'Ally! Look, it's Bruce and Sime, aren't they brill!'

'Yeah thrilling,' I replied cynically, while nibbling on what turned out to be a cucumber salad sandwich, ugh!

Placing my own binoculars to my eyes, I was unfortunately just in time to see a massive shark jump out of the waters and collect Sime in its huge jaws. As the monster belly-flopped back into the rollers, the seascape turned red with blood. Beach spectators began to scream in unison while the other horrified surfers scrambled, panic-stricken, to the shore.

Booby had fainted. His eyeglasses lay limply around his neck whilst the orange juice he had been drinking was wastefully draining onto the sand now adrift from his flaccid hand, but not before it had utilised his colourful shirt as a strainer. Looking at the ongoing scene, of course, I found the whole sight more fascinating than frightening. Then again, I was fifty metres or so away from the 'Carcharodon Carcharias' or for the less well-educated, the Great White Shark that was currently ripping the luckless Sime in half. My only sympathetic thought was, ouch that's gotta hurt!

The waters emptied quickly, and a number of surfers had fallen breathless onto the shore while their boards washed up, crashing unridden into the shallows. Booby had recovered a semblance of consciousness while the shark continued to thrash about in its feeding frenzy, spreading blood and guts about like a pissed-up Jackson Pollock. Booby didn't need the binoculars to understand what was going on and was straightaway in danger of another blackout.

What was going on here? It was too cold for a Great White or so we had thought and then the words of Sven the seagull resonated with me. He had indeed warned me that my presence would attract 'animals not normally seen hereabout' and that they would be 'visiting with malevolent hearts and thoughts'. And I remembered Pet Shop Pete's words:

'They are yours to command, only if you do not do so, they will assume you wish them to terminate those who do not honour you'.

It was then that I had my sledgehammer realisation - Fuck me! Jaws thinks he's on my payroll!

Pulling Booby to his feet and abandoning the picnic basket to the incoming tide, we made our way from the carnage. Men were shouting, women were crying, kids were screaming, not sure what the gender benders were doing. The event officials scampered about frantically, probably concerned that there might be a lawsuit in the offing. Booby was like a dead weight with his arm around my shoulder, you would have thought it had been him that had been sliced and diced in two. Unkindly, I reflected that at least he might have weighed less and been easier to transport. Once we'd reached the studio apartment, I hurled rather than assisted Booby to the sofa as I callously ignored his dying duck routine, 'Pull yourself together man!'

'Don't be hard on me Ally!' he whimpered. 'It's not every day you see a sweet young fellow bitten in half by a monster you know!'

I looked out through the apartment's open French doors at the unravelling scene below on the beach. It wasn't a monster, though it had been monstrous. I could communicate with the supernaturals yet I didn't know where to start with animals and clearly these fuckers had got the wrong end of the stick.

Within half an hour the shoreline was abandoned as a dark and thunderous sky rolled in along with waves that looked more in keeping with Hawaii than Cornwall. Moving out onto the balcony, I peered left toward the beach café. The staff were serving hot drinks to people shrouded in blankets, the whole scene looking like the aftermath of a bombing raid on the East End. Blue flashing lights bounced off the Tate Gallery's large glass frontage. Inspector Armstrong and Sgt Watts were scribbling down eyewitness accounts and two paramedics carried a stretcher up the beach. In its middle was a large bloody lump. No, the shark wasn't a monster, more like an endangered species way out of its natural environment and I knew I was going to need to get some specialist help.

'Go home Boobs. I need time and space to think.' I was short and to the point.

5.30am the following morning and I sat on the steps inside the external rotunda of the Tate Gallery, dusting the chalk off my hands and looking at the large magic circle I had cast on the concrete flooring with some pride. I had also placed four candles at equal points around this mystical ring and one in its centre. From this one, I lit my first cigarette of the day. Having inhaled deeply, I held the breath for a few seconds, closed my eyes, then exhaled slowly and started my chant:

'Praise Artio for your love of the beasts,
Such compassion and peace,
Humbled I am by your selfless love,
Guide me as I open my eyes, spirit and mind,
To the life of our sisters and brothers of the land,
Grant us your fullness – Your Kindness and Grace,
Come on down!'

I had used an ancient Celtic summoning spell, though that last bit was very much my handiwork. A mist appeared above the centre candle, extinguished summarily by a sudden gust of wind along with the other four. A spectral female voice echoed around the rotunda while the mist hovered tranquilly, 'Who calls the Goddess Artio?'

'Don't be shy lady, give us a butchers.' With that, a woman's form revealed itself. She was wearing a long green shroud-like dress. She was tall and powerfully built with an animal pelt that hung tightly around her shoulders like a cape and what appeared to be a bear's visage as a mask covering her face, all accentuated with long auburn hair trailing down to her waist. She reminded me of a scruffy Wonder Woman.

She aggressively repeated herself, 'Who calls the Goddess Artio?'

'You can call me Alex luv. I have a spot of bother that I am hoping you can help me with. I think it is in both our interests to sort it out double quick-you see.'

Drifting a little closer now, the silver torque around her neck in the shape of a snake biting its own tail reminded me of her Celtic pedigree, and then she spoke.

'I sense a dreadful natural imbalance, although I believe you are not of my religion magician?'

Scowling at her statement, I replied, 'It's more of a mythology darlin', it was never a religion was it really?'

Artio sat down cross-legged then issued her petition.

'You summoned me with the ritual of thanks, and I will demand payment for any assistance I provide conjurer, but of course you know this, so can I ask, is your gift prepared?'

Entering the circle and reaching out tentatively I assisted her to her feet and bravely held her close then continued, 'my 'gift' is available and will be more than worth your while, only its capture is the assistance I require.'

'So I can assume the imbalance is also caused by your 'gift' then? Tell me all.'

Well, I didn't leave anything out, sure she would have sussed me no sweat if I had tried anything underhand. Although it wasn't she who had entrapped Sven in the first place, I was counting on the fact that she, like IA, would not tolerate his attempted method of liberation. The devastation his attempt had already caused to the wildlife community must be beyond her patience. So, I made a deal with this Celtic goddess which was complex but no more than sensible and practical.

Once we had finished our parlay, Artio moved away and back to the centre of the rotunda and then facing me, arms extended and palms facing outwards, she swore an oath.

'I cannot tolerate the abomination you have described, and I know it to be true. Its cessation and its source shall be your 'gift' to me, Mr Crowley.'

Her arms lowered as she began to fade back into mist.

'Do as agreed then magician and we shall meet again at Godrevy Lighthouse one sunset hence. I will reassert my power there and then.'

And then she was gone, leaving only the faintest trace of vapour in her wake.

Booby wasn't going to be too happy about the deal I had made, but I guessed he had secretly always wanted to be a sailor and now he was going to get the chance. I had a saint on my side last time, I had a goddess this time.

The Sloop Inn does some lovely grub come lunchtime and Booby and I were sat enjoying our fare with a pint and a G&T, although I must admit the drinks weren't our first. In fact, I think it was fair to say we were a little the worse for wear. All around us the chatter was of yesterday's shark attack and even the Daily Mirror, open on the table next to ours had the headline, 'Cornish Jaws Strikes!'

There isn't normally much, that puts me off my food, but the arrival of Inspector Armstrong and his stupid sergeant ruined my appetite big time.

'Shit, what do these two fuckers want?' I blurted out a little too loudly.

'Shush Ally! Be careful, they'll run us in if they hear you,' came Booby's badly-timed warning.

The inspector put his boot up beside me on the bench probably trying to show off his concealed steel toe cap, a bit like a hooker adjusting her suspender belt. Looking directly at him I couldn't help myself.

'Don't tell me inspector? Big feet, big pricks?'

Straight away Sgt Watts chipped in aggressively, 'I'd like to see you try and make me laugh with that type of talk down the station. Fancy yourself as a bit of a comedian do you Crowley?'

He was asking for the abuse I dished back. 'You're a big enough joke on your own Cuntstable!'

The inspector had to restrain his subordinate once again as I emptied my pint with an accompanying guffaw. The inspector leaned closer in this time. His own temper appeared frayed as he whispered, 'don't push me Crowley. I am trying to remain sociable here.'

I should have conceded his demand, but the demon drink was having an uncivilised influence on my normally impeccable behaviour, 'Phooor Boobs, have you farted? Smells like pig shit around here,' and then before the inspector could retaliate, I followed on with a drunken apology and an invitation he would not have expected. 'Please forgive my mirth Captain… Have a pew.'

Seemingly off guard and a little taken aback by my generous offer, Armstrong sat alongside while Booby gawped bashfully at his still standing sergeant.

Gathering his thoughts, which didn't take long, he proceeded, 'We have had more than enough calamities and mishaps since you appeared on the scene, Mr Crowley. Only today we have had a dog pack attack on Fore Street, gulls by the hundreds dive-bombing innocent holidaymakers, rats running wild through the cinema and all this on top of yesterday's shark incident on Porthmeor Beach. Why is that do you think?'

Putting an index finger to my lips and looking as if I was going to impart a great secret, I placed my mouth close to the inspector's nearest ear. I cupped my hand to emphasise the fact that the information I was about to give was meant for him and him only and that it was also of a highly confidential nature. His eyes widened in anticipation and then I whispered in his shell-like, 'I fuckin' love you!'

I won't pretend the overnight B&B at the St Ives nick was a pleasant experience, although I do think the duty officer enjoyed my rendition of the old Englebert Humperdinck hit, 'Release Me' even though it was repeated throughout the night remorselessly as I noisily sobered up. I was just concluding the, 'Cause I don't love you anymore' line for the umpteenth time when the cell door opened and the constable, looking sideways at me in disgust, came straight to the point, 'OK Englebert sling your hook! Your boyfriend has bailed you out.'

As we walked away from the station Booby began, 'Blimey Ally, it's a good job you had all that cash stashed under the bed. I think they were hoping you wouldn't make bail and they could have kept you banged up for a bit longer. You should have seen that nasty sergeant's face when I coughed up the two grand!'

Putting my arm around my comrade, I thanked him, 'Cheers Boobs, you're a star. I knew you wouldn't let me down. Come on, we've got a job to do.'

And with that we were off to the pet shop.

Thirty minutes later and after a pleasant enough chat and hair of the dog, we exited Pet Shop Pete's gaff with a large cat box and made our way down to the harbour where a bit of banter and a small wad of cash saw us purchase an old fishing net from a local salty old sea dog. Our next stop was the anglers' store on the quay and I coughed up the considerable dough needed for a powerful fisherman's lantern and a couple of bright yellow wet weather suits complete with wellies that would have done Jacques Cousteau proud. Finally, with our equipment purchases complete, I sent Booby to arrange a motor boat hire agreement with the guy who normally catered for the harbour leisure boat day-trippers. A vessel was now ours whenever we wanted it, as long as the tide was in, that is! Once we had finished our suspicious commerce I was intrigued to see a large number of people trailing back up toward Street on Poll and being a nosy bastard at the best of times, decided it might be a good idea to find out what all the fuss was about.

Approaching the fine-looking Guildhall, I clocked the large sign outside, leaning contemptibly against Hepworth's Dual Form sculpture, which read in large red letters, 'Pubic Meeting Inside – All Welcome'. Well, it was either bad spelling or the event was going to be a lot more interesting than I could have hoped for down here in the wacky Wild West of Cornwall. Unfortunately, I was right the first time and seeing as it was only 2.15pm on a dullish day we were both soon inside, standing at the back amongst what was a bloody good turnout of the locals, who seemed to be up in arms.

Standing centre stage behind a tatty old lectern stood a tall, thin Ben Turpin lookalike, who I assumed was the mayor, factoring in the bulky gold chain which was way out of proportion and hung lifelessly around his scrawny neck. At his sides, seated like my old school teachers at a Monday morning assembly were obviously the great and the good of the town. These St Ives sycophants nodded their heads and shouted, 'Hear, Hear,' every time their civic boss made another pompous point. He certainly was loud enough, even from where Booby and I stood at the back. 'And I say it's not good enough! The Government needs to send in the Navy to patrol the coast to eliminate the sharks!' The crowd all cheered at that rash remark and once they had settled down again he timed the next part of his rant perfectly. 'We want the Army in to stop all these infernal animal attacks that have been occurring!' If that wasn't enough bile he finished this part of his speech with another unlikely and unrealistic call to arms. 'The RAF need to be summoned to halt all the terrible gull attacks. Now, now, now, I say!'

The audience reacted in unison with a loud hooray and as I lit a longed-for cigarette, I caught Booby with his hands to his mouth and standing balanced strangely on one leg as if he was playing the flute in Jethro Tull. At first I thought he was perhaps joining in with the general applause or was desperate for the loo, but however, soon realised as I looked downward, that he was cradling his face in terror as he watched a dozen hefty rats stream past our feet into the concentrated heart of the audience, completely unnoticed by the masses. 'Errrrrrrrr, vermin!' he squealed, although only I heard him, as the rest of the townsfolk and dignitaries were totally engrossed in the pomp and ceremony of the occasion.

The crowd were concentrating on the mayor's face so it was a shame none saw the foremost rat enter his left trouser leg at ankle level. He obviously didn't feel anything unusual either because he was so pumped up with his own importance and he continued, unaware with his bluster, 'our summer season will be devastated if action is not taken immediately!'

I watched the invading bulge make its way to just above his knee, 'I ask you all to stand firm and resolute, we cannot have anything or anybody disrupting our holiday bookings, our restaurant reservations, our cinema receipts,' up his thigh the lump continued its climb like Sherpa Tensing on speed as he continued in ignorance, 'Plus our farmers market and collectable fair takings are under threat.' You could tell the mayor was building up to a final shattering climax, but so too was the rat, as it moved into his groin area under cover of his baggy trousers. With his respectable be-speckled frump of a wife, who was the spit of Mary Whitehouse in her horn-rimmed glasses and twin-set, looking on admiringly and the rest of the audience spellbound by his impressive tirade, he wound himself up for the final push. 'Most importantly, we cannot let these events ruin our world-famous Summer…' I was watching his face as it turned into a spectacle of acute surprise and unbridled pain as the rat took a nasty bite out of his left testicle and he finished his sentence with a high pitched and poignant, '…. BAAAAALLS!'

The Guildhall had soon turned into a manic stamping party as the crowd screamed and panicked trying to rid themselves of the lighting quick pests underfoot. Booby and I had exited the public gallery, laughing like drains and there were a number of the rats following me like I was the Pied Piper, in some sort of unhealthy homage. The only thing entering the hall, amusingly, was the Black Manilishi, never one, it seemed, to miss an opportunity, and already with one struggling rat in his bloodied mouth.

It was getting toward the late afternoon and as it was bin collection day tomorrow it was time for Booby and me to make our move. Well, I must admit at this point Booby didn't really know what was going to happen. I knew he wouldn't let me down. By the time we approached the slipway at the head of Porthgwidden Beach, we had just about stopped giggling. We stood outside what was now an out of commission white painted public toilet. Booby knew enough about Sven's history to fill me in on the fact that this was where our seagull sculptor had lived and worked until the local council had turned him out and converted his studio into a public convenience. No wonder he was so bitter!

The good people of St Ives had on cue placed their large green wheelie bins out for the morning's collection and a couple were placed conveniently at the side of this ex-shithouse. 'That was the funniest thing I've seen in years back there Boobs,' I chuckled, trying to retain the light mood. 'Anyway, regardless, we have a little more comedy to enact I am afraid, and this is where you take star billing Mr de Faux, at the set-up stage of the proceedings.' I was secretly hoping that we would still be in one piece when we got to the punchline.

Ok, so now picture the scene. Boobs is sat on the low wall in front of the toilet block, he is leaning back against one of the stinky green wheelie bins. At his feet is the empty cat carrier and in his right hand he holds the most ginormous chocolate ice-cream cone. Yum, yum, yum! Out of the evening light arrives a seagull dive-bombing his unassuming prey. The sun is behind him, he is a virtuous kamikaze pilot. Then bang, the seagull strikes and the greedy bastard has the majority of the cone gripped vice-like in his beak before you can shake a stick. The ice cream explodes all over the shop, yet Booby bravely and as instructed, hangs onto his prize for grim life. While the wrestling is going on, I spring from my hidey-hole in the adjacent wheelie bin like a latter-day genie in a bottle and sling my recent fishing net purchase over Booby's head, trapping his ugly mug and the gull in an instant. 'Gotcha you bastard!'

It must have been a little claustrophobic being that close to the pecking, squawking gull yet I gathered the net even tighter around Booby's throat to make sure my avian friend couldn't escape and then looking directly into the gull's large beady eyes, I gave my instruction.

'Play it cool Sven and you won't get hurt. There's a good birdie!'

It was a simple task to extricate the bird from the net and my much relieved, ice-cream plastered, and sweating accomplice watched on in amazement as, holding Sven by his thick muscly neck, I forced him into the cat carrier closing the cage door behind him, and locking the security clips. 'Just be glad the Black Manilishi isn't in there with you!' I offered compassionately.

It must have looked an entertaining sight to the few straggling holidaymakers as, looking super smug, I led my shaking friend and accomplice along the back roads to the studio apartment with our captive seagull, pecking furiously at the wire cage bars in a forlorn bid for freedom.

It hadn't been hard for me to work out where Sven hung out, what with the council evicting him from his old gaff and then unceremoniously turning it into a toilet block. It all made sense, to me at least, that he wouldn't stray far from his old home and which was now his nest. The fact that I had observed that no other birds of any description went anywhere near that part of the town was the real giveaway.

Once we were back indoors, I placed the cat carrier on the table top and, looking at the irate gull through the bars, spoke directly to the bird.

'What was it you said Sven? Bit of a devil with an ice cream wasn't it? Hah, hah! Well you bit off more than you could chew this time my old cocker.'

And with that I threw a large bath towel over the carrier and educated the bird about the further trials he was to undergo that evening.

'Try and have a nap my old son, you will need all your energy tonight.'

Two hours later and it was just getting dark. Booby was peering miserably out of the front window at the rain which was coming in horizontally and battering the glass. Hoping, though not really expecting, that Booby had strong sea legs and a good constitution, I instructed him to put on the wet weather gear which I had purchased earlier in the day and I must say, we both looked the business in the traditional bright yellow waterproofs and sou'wester hats.

Minutes later, we were pushing our small rented motor boat out into the receding tide away from the centre of the picturesque harbour. It didn't, however, look too quaint on this evening as we rode the breakers out past Smeaton's pier into the grey and very choppy seas.

'Flipping heck! This is all a bit rough for a landlubber like me, I'm afraid Ally,' whinged the worried Booby.

'It'll give you the chance to experience the life of those poor bastards on the front cover of your book won't it,' I replied, knowing that my comments were hardly likely to compensate.

The sun was just kissing the waves on the horizon, so I knew it wouldn't be long before the lamp we had brought with us would be the only thing available to light our way, so gunning the outboard motor for all it was worth, I decided it was best to make haste while we still had enough light to avoid any rocks, and while I could still make out Godrevy Lighthouse in the distance, which I estimated to be about a mile away.

Booby acted as a reluctant lookout and with the cat carrier close to my feet, I held the rudder straight. Sven looked up through his bars and for the first time, tried to engage my attention. 'Let me out now Crowley and we can call it quits. What do you say old pal?'

With the wind in my face and the cold sea spray biting hard into my sense of humour, I kept my reply business-like. 'Old pal? Save it Sven. You tried to stitch me up, you bastard. I don't want your job mate, it doesn't come with any benefits I find attractive!'

He didn't try any chat during the rest of our short journey, knowing surely that I was a little bitter at his attempt to lumber me with all the pain and none of the gain he had suffered for the last fifteen years, as he had been reluctantly retained as IA's wildlife ambassador.

Passing the baton to me was his only chance to escape and I certainly didn't fancy that thankless task.

Booby was excitedly pointing at a small piece of sandy shoreline in-between some rocky outcrops as we approached the lighthouse rock, so I guided the boat in as gently as I could, intentionally running aground whilst attempting to avoid any damage, even though my vision was now totally lantern assisted as the sun had all but disappeared in a fog that had unhelpfully appeared from out of nowhere.

I had to shout. 'Grab the mooring rope Boobs and make us secure. Hopefully we won't be here too long and we don't want to swim back do we?' With that, I grabbed the cat carrier in one hand, the lantern in the other and jumped ashore like a pirate boarding a Spanish galleon. Booby was soon busy tying the rope to some vicious looking vertical rock spurs and fifty metres beyond him I noticed we were not alone, as another small boat was similarly housed.

'This should keep it safe, Ally,' confirmed Booby who had also noticed the other boat. 'Looks like we are not alone then, where are we going now?'

'Up to the lighthouse mate, to meet a goddess!'

Presently we were standing in the open doorway at the foot of the abandoned building, its high white walls towering above us steeply. Holding the lantern, I entered the illuminated entrance as Booby helpfully added to the ambience with his comments, 'Looks a bit spooky Ally!' Once inside, I placed the cat carrier on the dirt floor and was instantly aware of the two figures standing a dozen or so steps up the internal staircase. 'Good evening. Glad to see you both made it, then,' I declared.

Artio and Peter Green descended the slippery steps and were soon alongside myself and my fascinated companion as he stared almost rudely at the tall Celtic goddess and in particular, her bear's headdress and pelt cape.

Peter knelt down and, peering through the carrier bars at the captive gull, addressed the bird. 'Ah Sven! We meet again. I went to your funeral you know? I knew then it would take more than death to keep your soul at cease-fire though.'

The bird spoke in a dignified fashion, tinged with resentment.

'I would have loved some peace old man, but the saint trapped me here because of my worldly human animosities. She condemned me to stay forever, ensnared within this peninsula's boundary, a place that treated me with much disrespect and scorn and further burdened me, once she had transformed me into this winged monstrosity you see before you, with the unrealistic duty of responsibility for my animal brothers.'

He had a better grasp on the facts than he'd had on Booby's ice cream that's for sure!

It was a sad tale, only one that I had heard before so, without hesitation, I sprang the cage door and grabbed Sven again by his bulky neck, avoiding the sharply pointed beak.

'You tried to play tag with me, you crafty old buggar. Well, I'm afraid your still IT! And that's the way it's going to stay with the help of my errrm, associates here.'

Artio took my prompt and moved forward, placing her left hand upon the bird's head and issued her instruction, 'Hold him still Crowley, I will resolve his mind and remove all malice.' The gull's head morphed into Sven's human face. It looked like the extreme unction a priest would deliver to a condemned man. Artio closed his eyes with her fingertips. There was a translucent yellowish glow around the scene and it wasn't coming from the lantern. Booby caught my eye and asked innocently, 'Is this Black Magic Ally?'

I replied, although I looked to Peter for reassurance as I did so, 'No Boobs, think of this as more of the white stuff.'

Peter smiled shrewdly, appreciating the diplomacy of my answer, as I placed the stunned bird on the floor at the goddess's feet. 'I trust you brought your implement Mr Green? It's not that I don't trust Celtic practices, it's just that I would like a little insurance.'

Peter removed a large pair of scissors he had concealed in his coat pocket and snipping the air a couple of times for effect, he communicated his intention.

'I have done this to exotic birds in the past Mr Crowley, I am sure you have heard of clipping a bird's wings? Always to keep them safe you understand.' He didn't need my blessing, so he continued anyway, 'I have never done this to keep a whole town protected though.'

All this time, the seagull stood as if mesmerised at the centre of our formed circle, and he didn't flinch as Peter lifted him gently then, spreading each wing separately, made his expert cuts to the primary flight feathers. 'There Mr Crowley, it is done.'

Artio spoke like a High Court Judge delivering a verdict.

'This bird is just a bird again, magician. The inhabitants of this settlement are safe again and our ensnared soul is free and at peace at last. You can be assured our deal is concluded and that I am pleased with my 'gift'.'

I didn't really know what to say so I ham-fistedly mumbled in conclusion, 'jolly good.'

We cast off from our temporary moorings and into a night that was now becalmed and well-lit by a bright moon. Looking back at the lighthouse, the yellow glow was still shining bright at the entrance and although I had offered Artio a lift to the mainland, I was sure her sort travelled with far more grace and comfort than could be found on our modest ferry. Peter, already well ahead, had also reclaimed his on-loan cat carrier and as I lit my cigarette Booby piped up, 'It's a lovely night now Ally, isn't it?'

'Calm before the storm, perhaps my old mucker,' I replied and then I was back, locked in my thoughts.

What was left of Sven had a nice new home and a nice new owner to go with it. An owner who would take back the responsibilities that had been lost to her across time, as the Celtic goddess of wildlife. There would be plenty of fish for Sven to eat, although I was sure his diet of ice-cream and pasties was at an end, once and for all. With the tide right out now, Booby tied the mooring rope to an outlying buoy just outside of the harbour and we made our soggy way across the sands to the steps of Smeaton's Pier. Looking across the harbour from our vantage point once we had climbed the steps, I experienced an extraordinary sensation, well extraordinary for a gypsy like me anyway. This place was beginning to feel dangerously like home. The boats at sea curtsied on the now placid tides and Booby extinguished the lantern. There was only one thing we could do in the circumstances and looking at the bewildered face of my comrade in arms, I sounded the war cry, 'come on mate, let's go and have a pint!'

Part Four

A New King in Town

After a week or so of relative peace and quiet, I was lounging in the studio apartment watching the afternoon sewage on a large flat screen television that was fitted atop an old sea chest. Behind the screen one of Lucian's interior decorator acquaintances had strung up an old fishing net complete with colourful floats in an attempt at 'contemporised decoration'. It was not really my cup of tea as in all honesty, I would have preferred white blank walls with a couple of lifeless landscapes.

Booby had mentioned that there was a local interest programme scheduled for 3pm so I had settled down to have a butchers and bang on the button, it kicked off with a cute young newscaster, all tits and arse, plying her trade as she commenced her narration.

'An unprecedented period of horrific events has unfolded in the pretty seaside town of St Ives, Cornwall over the last few weeks.' The camera panned out and rather than just her body's best bits, the view expanded to include the familiar throngs of holidaymakers, taking in the picture postcard view of the harbour behind her. 'This has left the town reeling,' she continued, attempting a serious demeanour. 'It is, at this point, unclear what has led to these seemingly unrelated incidents.'

She paused dramatically and then a mug shot of Lillo Contattio polluted the screen, first a view from the front, which was bad enough, then another, sideways on, which was enough to frighten Dracula's bride. Behind him was the standard wall height indicator markings of the custody room and I chuckled to see he was only five feet, four inches. So much malice condensed into such an ugly little package! His old duelling scar was prominent, a diagonal slash across his face from right temple to left upper lip, fortunately, yet sadly it didn't spoil his looks! There were also more than a few cuts and scuff marks on his face, so I was pleased to see the porksters had given him a bit of a roughing up - all in the line of duty of course - during his recent capture.

The reporter recommenced her account.

'In the early hours of last Sunday morning, local resident and entrepreneur, Mr Lillo Contattio, was arrested following a disturbance at one of the town's most popular public houses, 'The Bizz'.

The picture on the screen now featured the smashed-up frontage of the aforementioned drinking den.

'He has been charged with multiple offences ranging from money laundering, living off immoral earnings, tax evasion, obtaining money or property or services through coercion and grievous bodily harm.'

That was all a bit of a mouthful, but I thought that last one was a bit harsh as how I understood it, the only harm he had done was to chip a police dog's incisor as it took a chunk out of his arse.

Next came a shot of the handsome but recently deceased Mr Bucca Dhu and she continued, 'Then a few days later, on a normally quiet evening in the town, another much respected businessman who amongst his other interests, owned the 'Bizz' public house, was murdered in front of a number of shocked witnesses in the Market Place by two previously esteemed, resident retailers, who have since it appears, fled the scene without trace.'

The screen was now split in two with a couple of nauseating domestic depictions of the creepy Phillip Browne and the ultra-smug Richard Soul. The pictures were quickly replaced by a panoramic view of an abandoned Porthmeor Beach, followed by a couple of stills showing the pandemonium of the shark attack and then the terrible film of the paramedics removing the blood-drenched stretcher from the sands. The reporter recommenced her narrative while the extracts continued.

'Before the citizens and holidaymakers of the town had a chance to catch their breath, a number of strange animal attacks occurred and on Saturday afternoon during the UK Surfing Championships, which was held in front of the world-famous Tate gallery on the beautiful Porthmeor Beach, a most improbable and unprecedented shark attack claimed the life of a much loved Australian lifeguard, Mr. Simon Hough.'

The next section of footage at least brought a smile back to my face at the memory, as the film crew crammed in around the mayor who lay in his hospital bed with a blanket covering the surgical cage that protected his nether regions, presumably preventing the one ball he had left intacto, sticking to the crisp white sheets. I wasn't certain, but it looked like the detached other testicle was pickled in a jar on his bedside table alongside his Ribena. Miserably, it didn't seem as if anybody had bothered to bring him in some grapes.

The reporter continued to be filmed at his side while he gurned.

'Even the town's honourable mayor was attacked by a crazed common rat that bit him as he made an impassioned speech regarding the recent events at a public meeting at the Guildhall.'

She then thrust her microphone into his face, expectant, it seemed, of some sort of scoop. The mayor spoke in a strained manner, clearly, but unhelpfully under the influence of his morphine drip.

'Th, the, this sort of thing is beyond the pale. Although I have lost my left testicle, the town's businesses stand to lose a whole lot more, I am afraid to say.'

Fucking capitalist to the end! My red flip flop bounced off the mayor's bald-headed onscreen image as I made my own contribution to the programme before pushing the off switch, 'wanker!'

Eyeing the contents of the fridge, I realised that I was running low on supplies. Where had Booby got to? Replacing my discarded flip-flop, I pulled the front door to behind me, lit my cigarette and started up the incline intending to top up my provisions. Rounding the corner at the top of the back road, I spotted the AWOL Booby sitting on the wall at the side of the

Norse Stores and as I got closer, noticed two suitcases either side of him. It looked like he had been crying.

'What's going on here mate?'

My monosyllabic enquiry startled him back to reality and he lifted his red, puffy, tear-stained face that was full of sorrow to answer dejectedly, 'I've been slung out Ally, what am I going to do?'

At first, Booby didn't want to confront his landlady, but after a little bullying, we both walked up to the small cottage guest house that was his rented home and I rapped hard on its front door. Waiting for a reply, I took a gander at the nameplate which specified in a Celtic font, 'Trivago's Guest House'. Underneath it hung a 'Vacancies' sign. Booby had retreated back a number of paces, eyeing the entrance apprehensively as I rapped even harder a second time, whilst taking a long drag. A rather attractive, but snotty piece of work answered the door. I judged her to be early forties and detected straight away that the ample bosom on show had probably been enhanced. She lowered her glasses seductively with her long thin manicured fingers and made it sound like she was doing me a favour as she asked in her posh voice, 'Can I help you?'

'I take it you're the landlady darlin'? Tamsin isn't it?'

Slowly she removed her glasses, dropping them level with the hem of the skimpy skirt she was nearly wearing.

'Lady Tamsin Trivago to you my man. I am the proprietor, if that is what you mean. What is it exactly you want, Mr Errrrr?'

'Crowley darlin, but you can call me Alex if you like,' and with that I pushed past her and made my way through to a small hallway. 'You can drop the airs and graces as well Mrs Snotty Knickers!'

Her ladyship followed me through to her lounge, predictably both tidy and spacious.

Indignantly she screeched, 'Just who the bloody hell do you think you are barging in here like that? I am a town councillor and my husband is a man of some repute and a member of the House of Lords to boot!'

She nearly blew a gasket as she watched me trample my dog-end out on what was probably a very expensive handwoven rug.

'I couldn't give a monkeys luv! Now stick the kettle on, there's a good girl.'

Let's just say it wasn't long before I was standing back on the street, but I did at least have Booby's deposit money and the rest of the rent he had paid in advance, plus of course a little compensation for the lack of notice. It seemed she had lobbed him out because of his association with yours truly. Seemed also I was raising a few hackles with the town's blue bloods. I wedged the cash into Booby's shirt pocket and then, reaching around him, picked up his suitcases. They were sadly a little on the light side, although they probably contained every possession he owned.

'Come on son, let's get you settled in with me.'

It was the very least I could do.

We walked back to the studio apartment along the Porthmeor Beach promenade and it was disquieting to see that the shoreline had barbed wire barricades in place to stop folks going into the sea. A few military looking types were patrolling and there were a couple of signs declaring, 'Off Limits' and 'Danger'. It looked like a film still out of 'The Great Escape' and I half expected Steve McQueen to appear and attempt a motorcycle jump at any minute. The shark had long gone, but there was no way for the town's councillors and law enforcement bods to know that, I supposed.

It was obvious that I was now, 'persona non grata' and poor old Booby's copybook had been blotted irrevocably due to our friendship, a friendship that I was more than a little grateful for and one that I would protect at all cost.

Back at the studio, Booby whipped up our evening banquet looking overjoyed in his new home. It wasn't hard to work out who had spread the poison and it smelt of pig, so I determined there and then to repay the compliment.

It was dusky enough to conceal my movements from any prying eyes, though just light enough for me to observe the sneaky Inspector Armstrong knocking at the Trivago Guest House front door. Peeking from behind a granite cottage corner, I could see that he was looking dubiously around, to make sure he hadn't been spotted. He had a guilty secret written all over him. The door opened and Lady Tamsin leered sexily at her apparently anticipated visitor. She obviously had a job around the house or at least in the bedroom that needed seeing to and she certainly seemed more pleased to see him than she had been to see me. As he entered quickly, it was clear that it wasn't a pistol he had in his trouser pocket! It always amazes me that members of a profession that relies so heavily on logic and predictability can so easily be caught in their own net. It hadn't taken much digging down the Sloop earlier that evening, to unearth a few rumours about the inspector and Lady Muck. Neither was well liked, and it seemed, any exposé would be a welcome and entertaining diversion for the hoi polloi.

There wasn't any security to speak of at the guest house, so it was a simple matter of popping over the back wall and onto the conveniently placed shed roof. My exertions didn't even cause me a shortage of breath. To be fair, I even took my time to finish a cigarette, casting the dog end into the darkness before I stood upright on the apex. It produced instant gratification and amusement to see the events taking place through the bedroom window, as the inspector and Lady Muck were going at it like knives!

'Be prepared!' my old Cub Scout leader Akela always used to say and that advice had always stood me in good stead, so I attached the mobile phone to the window pane with some gaffer tape. I didn't think that there was much chance of them noticing the red recording light of the phone's camera function, as long as the inspector didn't shoot his load too early. I was further assured that there wouldn't be a premature ejaculation as I heard her muffled voice proclaim, 'Oeeeeeeeeeer! That's nice daddy, do it to me again, you brute!'

Down safely on terra firma and ambling away unperturbed, I made the pre-arranged call on my supplementary mobile phone, using the kind of language my geek friend would appreciate. 'Marco! You ready mate? You're my Hi-fi, Wi-Fi, Bluetooth Soothsayer! You're the man! You know what to do so hook them up and go to it buddy. I owe you one mate. Catch you soon, toodle pip.'

I had just enough time to make it back down to the Sloop and I was pleased to see that the arsehole on legs that was Sgt Watts was enjoying a pint in the corner, not unsurprisingly on his lonesome. The trouble with pubs today is that there's a television on every wall which means you can't help but watch them. Whatever happened to the good old jukebox blaring out Smoke on the Water or Freebird or, better still, Whole Lotta Love, eh?

It wasn't hard to imagine the rest of the town's populace huddled around their screens either, enjoying Corrie or some other alternative shite on the Beeb. I only just had time to have a small sip of my purchased pint of Rattler when the town's multiple television screens went all fuzzy, bang on cue. The electrical cackle caused by the new foreign signal interruption, courtesy of my old mucker Marco, drew everyone's attention and the soap opera melodrama was replaced by a perfectly framed Inspector Armstrong servicing her ladyship from behind doggy-style and all at an impressive seesaw pace I must say. I was surprised he had it in him, but I was more astonished that a creature like her would let him put it in her!

Sgt Watts was choking as his lager had returned from his gullet and exited his nostrils in shock as he watched with watering eyes, his boss ploughing on like a trick dog totally unaware of his appreciative large local audience. Once Watts had finished his initial choking fit, he was on his handset, and we all watched on screen as the impressive inspector answered without too much disruption at his end. 'Boss! Boss!' He exclaimed, 'Pull it out and get down! You've been framed!'

A couple of days later, crack of sparrow's fart apparently, Inspector Armstrong stood to attention in front of his Chief Constable, George Hallam, who as the officious oaf he was, remained seated behind his large, leather-topped office desk as he pontificated.

'I should be asking for your warrant card Inspector Armstrong. You have brought this force into considerable disrepute.'

'Yes Sir.'

There was of course no credible defence for the hapless porkster. The Chief deigned to lift his eyes up to Armstrong and he continued disapprovingly, 'I played golf with Lord Terrance Trivago yesterday afternoon and I can tell you he was none too impressed to see her ladyship on her hands and knees featured on the clubhouse television while our party were all enjoying the nineteenth hole.'

The interview hadn't lasted long by all accounts and the Chief Constable looked out of his office window to observe Armstrong bounding down the Police Headquarters front steps to a waiting car driven by the ever-faithful Sgt Watts. I think they were both keen to pay me a visit, but they weren't intending to pick up any flowers on their way!

The Chief Constable was quickly on the dog and at the other end of the line, unbeknown to me at the time, the fat, portentous and vicious aristocrat that was Lord Terrance Trivago answered the call from his opulent House of Lords surroundings. The conversation was apparently brief and to the point. 'Yes, that's good to know, Your Lordship,' said the toadying Chief Constable, 'I am sure your eradicator will be able to rid us of this unwelcome occultist quickly and cleanly. I must agree and am sorry to say that I don't think my own men are up to that task anymore.'

The conversation's conclusion was both sickening and decisive as His Lordship proceeded to wind up. 'No, that has become obvious my dear Chief Constable.

In fact, this Inspector Armstrong has also enjoyed my wife's errrm, entertainment for the last time. I am sure I can trust you to clean up any mess my man leaves? Discreetly of course, I will be more than appreciative George.'

With that ringing in his ears and a smile beaming from one to the other, the Chief Constable replaced the handset and spoke to himself aloud, 'Sir George Arthur Hallam. It has a certain ring to it if I say so myself. Hah, hah, hah.'

Lord Terrance was clearly as hi-tech savvy as I was, and from his office, he had then spoken immediately by video link to another unlikely character. 'Your Majesty, the preparations have been concluded. I am sure you will wish to unseat this pretender as soon as is possible?' Lord Terrance viewed the man on the screen in front of him, he was distinguished looking and fully bearded. A bit of a cross between Richard the Lionheart and a Wall Street banker, decked out in a wide lined pinstriped three piece suit.

The answer came back in a strong and calculated tone, 'Correct Lord Terrance. I succeeded King Arthur himself and I can assure you that this upstart will not supplant me. He may share my charisma, but he will never share my kingdom. Thank you for bringing him to my attention.'

Lord Terrance replied, undoubtedly impressed and grateful. 'My pleasure Your Highness. Can we expect you shortly?'

The noble adjusted his posture and re-joined the conversation in his own good time, 'Before long, Sir Terrance, before long. The cover of darkness has been always an advantage worth corruption. Goodbye my friend, I will not forget you.'

And with that, the screen filled with static and faded.

Lord Terrance sat back and placed his hands together, not about to pray, rather in contemplation.

'Well, well, well, King Constantine himself! I never knew these things existed until I was invited to join the Lodge. Hah! I don't fancy our trickster's chances much against him.'

Obviously, I was not aware of any of this malarkey at the time. Rather, I was sat happily with Booby, at Maggie's enjoying coffee and cakes. Peering through the window at the midday sunseekers, I observed Inspector Armstrong in the passenger seat while Sgt Watts driving like a poor man's Sterling Moss on a hill climb, accelerated up the incline in their unmarked cop car, apparently on their way to pay me a friendly visit. My thoughts came with a smile as I had another mouthful of cake. Not at home today guys, so please call again, hah, hah!

'This is beautiful devil's food cake Ally. Its soooooo rich! Much better than your average chocolate offerings don't you think?'

I couldn't argue with Booby's appraisal and as Maggie cleared away the plates I was worried that if he swallowed any more, he would explode. I don't know what notch his belt was on but I was sure it wasn't the same as the one he had started out with that morning.

'I think we'd better walk this off Boobs, we need a few supplies anyway.'

It wasn't strictly true, but I thought it best to get him moving before he had a heart attack or a stroke.

A couple of times around the town and then with Booby laden with plastic shopping bags and me on my third cigarette we found ourselves walking slowly down the back road to the studio yet again. On the corner licking his paws was the Black Manilishi and he soon joined our gentle descent and was at the door uninvited well before we were.

As Booby boiled the kettle, I looked out to the beach and I guess you could call it instinct, I knew trouble was on its way. The barbed barricades looked out of place on the sands as the holidaymakers peered through them and out to sea, hoping perhaps to see a fin or two? I knew it would take more than a little razor wire to get in the way of whatever was coming to sort me out though. Reassured, I looked at the cat and thought about IA. Thankfully I had friends in high places, and I didn't doubt that I would need her help again this summer.

Booby looked on confused as I drew the protective signs and sigils that he could not have been expected to recognise, all over the apartment walls, doors and windows. He probably thought innocently enough that I had been inspired by the cultural surroundings of the art colony, yet he knew better than to ask. He was even more fascinated when I lit seven candles all in the middle of the table, though again he kept his beak sensibly shut. I didn't know exactly what was coming, but I did know that it wasn't going to be pleasant. I supposed I had pissed a few of the local aristos off and they were the types to have connections that could prove bothersome. With the illustrative fortification works complete, I felt naively that I would at least be safe in the studio apartment, as long as I wasn't flushed out into the open.

Booby was rearranging the contents of the fridge as the house telephone started to ring so I thought I would do him a favour and get off my arse to answer it.

'Ah Clouseau!' It was Inspector Armstrong. 'I thought you might call. Sorry I wasn't in earlier. Probably a good job for your sake though.' Then rudely I snorted like a pig. I couldn't so much hear the abuse from the other end of the line as feel it. I threw myself laughing down onto the sofa still clutching the handpiece, 'No, I don't suppose you did find it amusing, old bean.' Then I sat upright and put my serious head on, 'Take my advice son. You and your trained monkey would do best to give me a wide berth.'

On his mobile like a secret squirrel just up the road and around the corner from the studio, Armstrong superficially agreed, 'OK Crowley, let's call it a truce hey? How about a drink tonight to seal the deal, no hard feelings and all that?'

It wasn't convincing, but I played along anyway, 'That would be delightful Inspector. The Union at nine then. Ciao baby!'

With the call concluded, Inspector Armstrong had apparently turned sharply to his sidekick and with a vicious look in his eyes, given instruction that I was later to discern.

'Go get a couple of body bags from the nick will you sergeant.'

Two hours later and one of the larger carrier bags that Booby was trying to accommodate unsuccessfully in the fridge displayed its logo prominently - 'St Ives Butchers'. It was full to the brim and solid looking and contained our Sunday joint.

'Don't put that away Boobs, I like it nice and bloody. Oh, and by the way, did you manage to get hold of your mate the biker, and arrange my companions for tonight?'

It had already passed nine o'clock as I revelled along Fore Street on the way to the boozer and my pre-arranged rendezvous with the filth. I had an arm each around two of the meanest looking cycle sluts you could ever wish to meet. They were all fanny pelmets, stripper heels, leather jackets and skin that wouldn't have looked out of place on a rhino. It was only twilight now at this time of year, but these were the type of birds you would not have wanted to be seen with in broad daylight.

'Thanks for coming girls, I'm sure we're going to have a great time.' I said to the one called Suzy.

'We alus has a good time dearie! I hope you got plenty of dough then for me an Pearl?'

She laid her modus operandi out succinctly.

Turning my head toward the other vixen and trying hard not to set her Bonnie Tyler hair sprayed to buggery barnet alight with my cigarette, she joined in,

'Yeah, we isn't cheap you know my luver. We like the bestest things in life, me an Suz!'

Both of them needed a good sandblasting more like. Regardless, I bowled loudly into the Union as the seated holidaymakers looked on a little disconcerted, but carried on with their drinking and eating irrespective, with the finest British 'stiff upper lip' resolution. Sgt Watts was sat inside the closest so I addressed him maliciously, 'Two G&Ts, a pint of lager for me and a cider dash for your guvnor. Oh, and get yourself a Coca Cola sonny boy, ha, ha, ha!'

He made his way to the bar without rebuff, admirably holding his temper, but being a competent lip reader, I registered the, 'I'll swing for that fucker!' he made inaudibly to his boss.

St Ives' pubs are lively at the best of times and this night was no different. It was like a German Bierkeller complete with quite a few Germans judging from the guttural articulation I was hearing. Even Sgt Watts joined in the revelry, though he couldn't help being a twat, 'Where's your bent mate Crowley? Doing his nails I bet! Hah, hah!'

'Doing yours for your coffin more like,' I replied as the clock on the wall passed 10.30pm. 'Actually, he's on the phone tonight ringing an old friend he used to ride his bike with.'

I wasn't sure what Watts visualised, although I was pretty certain it was nothing like the scene now being played out back at the studio apartment as Booby was pompously imparting his information and instructions down the blower.

'Yes, that's right Chopper, The Union and I should hurry up if I were you!'

Ten miles away, out towards Lands' End in a broken-down old wreck of a cottage block, Chopper the leader of the biker gang looking all hot, sweaty and unhealthy in his filthy cut-offs, bellowed out his instructions to the rest of his posse as they lay around lethargically. 'Saddle up me boyos! The birds are about to chow down on some pork, an' we can't be avin' that now's can we?' Less than a minute later it was all systems go as the bikers thundered away from their dosshouse, headed for St Ives, all smoke and thunderous racket.

The first chair exited the pub window about ten seconds after Boobs and I had departed. As Chopper and his motley crew had come in we'd left, as the evening had turned a little tedious to say the least. Still, it looked like it was warming up a bit now as the crashing of furniture and the smashing of glasses ramped up nicely.

'They won't kill them will they Ally?' Booby wondered worriedly.

I wasn't really sure to be honest, yet I tried to allay his fears anyway.

'No, no, no mate, just a few life-changing injuries at worst I would imagine. I wouldn't feel too sorry for them though, considering what they had planned for you.'

And with that I dropped the two body bags I had snatched from beneath the porksters' table onto the cobbles. Booby looked down at them trying to comprehend what they were, as I looked up into the now pitch black sky. The wind had picked up and it blew in warmly from the sea as I watched the rubbish on the stones turn in unnatural circles. I knew it was time to get indoors, behind my protection trappings, as something felt very wrong.

Once inside I felt safer, that is until I had a butchers out onto the beach and there, no more than thirty feet away on the shore, stood a tall bearded geezer in a fuck you pin-striped suit. I hadn't put the light on when we had re-entered the studio, though I understood instantly that this bastard didn't need his eyes to realise I was at home, and as I dismissed that thought, Booby innocently flipped the wall switch and lit the place up like Blackpool Illuminations. I must have been well backlit now as I moved out onto the balcony, but I decided it was best to play it cool and lit my cigarette, contemptuously throwing the spent match out onto the beach. My voyeur hadn't moved, he just stood and stared. He looked distinguished and I couldn't quite place him. He raised his arm and pointed up toward my vantage point. Like a gun, his index finger seemed to line up precisely with my temples. The best I could do in return was to flick him the finger and walk coolly away from the French doors. My protection must have worked, otherwise he would have been all over me like a rash by then.

Booby hadn't clocked any of this thankfully and before he could kick his shoes off and settle in for the night I instructed him forcefully, 'Go back to the Union Boobs. Get on the back of Chopper's bike and get the fuck out of here tonight!' He stood there looking confused and crestfallen, so I followed up with a high decibel, 'Go!' which did the trick.

The door caught by the wind slammed shut behind me as he left and I pushed the numbers on the telephone keypad. Rule number one according to Sun Tzu's Art of War is, 'Know your enemy,' so less than a mile away the pet shop telephone began to ring in reaction.

The voice at the other end of the line answered clearly.

'Hello Mr Crowley, I was expecting your call.'

'Cut the crap Peter, who the fuck is he?' I demanded, to which he replied, 'I won't bother with the small talk then. He is King Constantine, a sixth-century type, all battle-axe and brawn I am afraid to say. You're on his manor, Mr Crowley. You must have made some powerful enemies and it seems they have been busy with the spell work to summon him up.'

I could hear the birds twittering in the background as he continued and as I regarded the beach for a second time I could see my adversary had indeed transformed out of his suit and now looked very much the Celtic warlord Peter had described.

'He will try to flush you out into the open Mr Crowley and then probably get a grip on your windpipe! These chaps are very old school you know.'

The king raised his arm to the sky and on his command the heavens lit up with a flash of lightning following a super heavyweight rumble of thunder. Long since, not really concentrating on Peter's words, I vaguely remember hearing him inquire if I was still on the line. Instead of the polite answer he deserved, the handset was dropped to the hard floor as I could only stand transfixed regarding the call display legend I had flippantly programmed in previously, 'Pet Shop Pete.'

Nearby, at the Island's summit, as it was later recounted, a mere stone's throw from the small St Nicholas Chapel, the evening's events were also being witnessed by the two aged National Coast Watch Institution volunteers, Derek and Joan Panalba, who were pulling the ten-till-six shifts. They were dressed smartly in their uniforms, complete with golden shoulder epaulettes, which was all part and parcel of the proud job this dedicated couple had done together as a husband and wife team for many years. Derek, white-bearded and a lookalike for the famous Captain Birdseye character, was looking at his radar monitor as it scanned the horizon electronically, piercing the storm that had sprung from nowhere.

'Blimey Joan! Says there's a fifty-footer out there girl. Come from nothing an' it's only a mile off an' heading ours way fast!'

'Do you think it will make landfall Derek?' asked his gentle wife as she looked up from her knitting, instantly losing track of her pattern.

Derek had moved quickly to the front screen of the station house and peering through his retirement gift binoculars, as the night sky lit up with yet another lightning strike, the massive wave stood proud on the seascape. 'Bloody hell Joan! Best sound the alarm nows!'

It was the fastest Joan had moved in years, she could see her husband wasn't kidding her this time and all the hours of training paid off in spades as she pushed the big red button on the station wall marked, 'Wave Alarm'. Instantly the sea horns sounded out loud and proud like an air raid warning.

The wave had arrived quickly at the head of the Island and looked ready to break hard on the seashore. Its height was at least equivalent to where I now stood looking amazed out of the French doors and the king stood laughing like a maniac as the wave absorbed his figure on its passing. I knew then that I hadn't seen the last of him though, and I felt an unlikely remorse, realising that it wouldn't just be me that would be 'flushed out' when the waters tore through the beach fronted properties. I wondered how many innocent people would be swept up in this grudge match, and then, whoosh, the wave struck with all its mighty force, collecting me up like a rag doll as it crashed in through the apartment. It swept me along with every unfixed stick of furniture straight through the entrance way along to the front door, which I accumulated and opened by my headfirst impact outward onto the path. My neighbours and I, along with all their worldly goods were forced further up the sloping backstreets and even as the power of the wave diminished slowly, it occurred to me that this king had indeed used a hammer to crack a nut.

Trying desperately to stay afloat, only in a somewhat dazed state, I cried out with both my arms held aloft, 'IAaaaaaaaaaaa!' The best way to stop a demon I had decided was to call my guardian angel, although it was more in hope than certainty that she would indeed answer my cry and come to my aid. Thankfully from the pitch sky the saint swooped down into the broiling waters, plucking me from my disastrous circumstances. Again she was impressively decked out in full battle dress as she placed me, choking and wringing wet, in the small Norway Square at the top of the incline, as that had been the furthest the wave had breached, and pushed me, before it had turned back on itself, making it's just as destructive way back towards the beach, washing everything in its wake back down the slopes in a frantic return visit demolition.

Pulling myself up onto my elbows, I was confronted with the sight of the medieval fiend, who was out to finish the job that his tidal wave had started, standing at the entrance to the square. He held a nauseating looking mace in his right hand and the vicious, dented spiked ball swinging on the end of its chain looked like it had seen plenty of action in the past.

Crouching like a tiger waiting to pounce, he made his declaration of war, 'I would make you beg charlatan, only you are beneath my contempt! There can only ever be one king of this peninsula.'

He didn't look much like he wanted to debate things any further as he moved heavily and aggressively toward my still prone form, not that I thought it was worth the effort trying to persuade him of the folly of his ways.

Just as he began to draw back his weapon, taking up his death stroke pose, IA landed between us.

'And only one Saint, Dark King!' she announced, as she unleashed a flare from her broadsword. Stopped dead in his tracks, he began to shy away like a pantomime villain, illuminated by the yellow hellfire glow I had witnessed in the church. He covered his eyes and ears with his forearms and began to stagger in pain. As the agony overtook the medieval monarch, I looked on in astonishment. He fled into the darkness and it occurred to me that the Ace in the pack that was IA had trumped a king.

'Th, th, thank you.' My appreciation was not enough. She had already gone. I was certain that I wouldn't get away with that trick again, realising instantly that I had better start cooking up a plan B, because I was also sure that my aggressors wouldn't give up or leave it at that.

At daybreak, the tide was right out, and I stood looking from the beach up at the huge sand ridges with broken barricades and razor wire sticking out like Christmas tree decorations that had been driven violently into the seafront cottages. I soon became aware of the petite yet powerful figure that appeared beside me.

'You saved my life last night IA, how can I repay you?'

She was now dressed in her twenty-first century guise, complete as always, with large backpack.

'I cannot permit this king continued entry to my protectorate, it took centuries to rid ourselves of his pagan type. Be aware though magician, I cannot intervene personally again.'

I couldn't look at her directly for fear of showing my emotions, though it was doubtful she would have noticed anyway, as she continued to view the mayhem in front of her. It was my turn to set things straight.

'I understand that my presence here has enticed a number of pests and the like and I suppose you are here to make it plain that it is my responsibility to remove them. That right luv?'

Turning to her, expecting a simple confirmation, her image had gone and her physical presence was replaced by a sweet old lady holding out a styrene cup full of strong tea. She was even smaller than IA and she introduced herself as 'Mrs Joan Panalba,' and considerately inquired, 'is you all righty my dear? Must 'ave been a bit of a shock, I bets. Me an' Derek has never seen anything like it, damn near swept us off the Island it did!'

Her husband had now joined us along with a few of my newly homeless neighbours who hovered around inspecting the damage done, shaking their heads in disbelief.

'That was a real freak wave boy!' exclaimed the elderly watchman. 'They calls 'em Rogues, come from nowheres, outs of nothing and then smashes into you, an' then is gone. All in a matter of a few minutes. Wham! Bam! Thank you, ma'am!'

He then pointed up into the sky, obviously a God-fearing man and continued, 'It's as if The Almighty has used it as a weapon.'

I, of course, knew it was as far as you could get from an Act of God, being more one of his fallen angels.

Joan and Derek guided me gently away off the beach and up onto the dry grass of the Island's slopes, where the rest of the survivors sat around with blankets draped over their shoulders. These innocent victims were surrounded by members of the local community who generously fed and watered them and who were also attending to any cuts and bruises. No one had been killed, thankfully, just a few broken bones at worst, only I couldn't help feeling guilty having brought this plague down upon these guiltless folks' heads.

Once I had thanked my elderly helpers, I walked back down the sand-swept back streets and into the doorway of what was left of the studio apartment. The door itself was lying like a drunk slumped against the wall waiting to wake up before he pissed his pants. The footsteps behind me announced the timely return of my housemate. 'Oh my god Ally! What has happened here?'

'Had a visitor Boobs,' was all I could manage.

We were going to need somewhere to stay for a bit until I could get the repairs sorted. With a couple of bin bags full of sodden clothes and belongings, which in both cases was not a lot thanks to our recent wash out, we were both stood out on the front doorstep of Trivago's Guest House. Fortuitously pigs hadn't flown and we had also salvaged the Sunday joint in the plastic butcher's bag.

Lady Tamsin stood with her arms crossed. She had opened the door with a 'fuck off' type posture. This was cosmetically offset by the nasty looking black eye and long, thin plaster above her left eyebrow. 'You must be joking,' she blurted out, however, I wasn't one to hang around outside, so barged in past her.

'Never been more serious in all my life darlin', although, we wouldn't want your hubby, his Lordship, knowing would we?' Her shiner was horrendous and I couldn't help staring at it as I carried on pointing out the facts, 'it doesn't look like you owe him much respect does it anyway?'

A comically resigned look came over her face and taking that as his prompt, Booby followed me into what he considered his real home.

'We only need the one room luv, for Boobs. I'm happy to share with you!'

I waited for an explosion, though none came and Booby bounded up the stairs keen to unpack. I followed unflappably upward and without looking, asked the surprised aristocrat over my shoulder while she stood watching at the foot of the stairs aghast, 'Which room we in your ladyship? I need a bath, been a long, smelly night. Come and scrub my back, will you?'

Five minutes later I was well up to my neck in an over-warm bath in an equally over-fragrant bathroom, enjoying a long overdue cigarette, another thing I had ponced, as my own stash was a little soggy to say the least. The rhythmic tap, tap, tap on the bathroom door was a nice touch considering it was her house. 'Come in darlin', it ain't locked,' and with that there she stood, naked as a new-born baby but a whole lot less innocent, complete with a sponge in one hand and a bottle of champagne and two of her finest flutes in the other.

'Well, you did ask!' were her last words before I reached out and pulled her into the tub with me.

I fucking hate the majority of library staff and the St Ives branch was no different. They fart-arsed around pretending to do everything other than what they were getting paid for, which in my mind was to put the books on the shelves in the right order. It was apparently getting close to closing time and the snotbag in a green floral dress and cowboy boots that made her look like a horticultural cowgirl, milled around in the background as I sat in the 'Reference Area'. My trench coat was hanging over the back of the chair I had occupied for the last five hours, looking unseasonably out of place as my involuntary dip in the Atlantic had chilled me to the bone. My reputation in the town was now at a level that ensured none of the staff had the bottle to attempt a reprimand as I smoked my way through a full packet of cigarettes and guzzled my way through a bottle of Jack as the afternoon progressed.

The reference books had supplied me with enough knowledge and understanding of the local Celtic mythos and peninsula history to enable me to cut the wheat from the chaff. Now I was nearly ready to use all of my new gained understanding and plot the tactics needed to safeguard my existence and plan the attempt to eliminate this recent regal threat. I didn't think that a parlay would work, yet as long as I could appeal to the king's undoubtedly massive ego, I was sure he would at least attend one. All I needed was a broker to get the invite out.

'Ding-a-Ling-a-Ling-a-Ling' sounded the doorbell as I tripped into the pet shop. Peter was standing wearing a rather colourful skull cap and was clumsily pouring birdseed into a cage feeder, with the majority of it landing on the floor at his feet. He didn't even have to look at me as he began, 'Ah, Mr Crowley, I wondered how long it would take you to visit me again.'

If he thought I was going to show him how impressed I was with his instinctive assumptions he was badly mistaken, so I thrust a scrappy piece of paper toward him. 'Here are the co-ordinates. I want you to set a meeting up for me with our wrathful royal, my old son. I think he has gotten the wrong end of the stick and I need to errr, enlighten him.'

Peter looked disapprovingly over the rim of his spectacles and dispensed his sensible advice. 'Surely, I can contact your royal foe, but it is dangerous work for me and bloody suicidal for you Mr Crowley. Do you really think you can enlighten the incarnation of a medieval tyrant who once killed children inside a church?'

It was a fair question, one to which I already knew the answer, having studied his form at the library earlier. It was also clear that I would be seen only as bait for any suggested rendezvous and not as some sort of diplomat who wanted to discuss a compromise when none was possible. I was positive this king had only one outcome in mind and that involved using his ball and chain on my cranium. The only chance I had was in the selection of our battleground, a selection I was positive he wouldn't twig, driven more by his arrogance than cautioned by any good sense he might possess.

'Give me a bell Pete, best of luck pal, speak soon,' I called over my shoulder as, thanks to his twee door alarm, I musically left his shop.

Luckily, I had managed to have a little nap that afternoon once her Ladyship had stopped bouncing all over my bones and when I awoke to the sound of the telephone ringing, it was time for tea. Tamsin was curled around me all lovey-dovey like, and as I picked the 1930s Duchess telephone receiver off the bedside table, she began to wake fully, rather too contentedly I thought. I peered out into the darkening night through the bedroom curtains.

'Cheers Pete. I appreciate the risk you have taken pal. I owe you one. Tell him I'll see him midnight at Lanyon Quoit then.'

I knew by the tone of Peter's voice that he was not alone. He told me later that King Constantine had sat opposite him, unperturbed in his pinstriped suit, all arrogant and aloof while he made his call to me, making sure, as best he could, that there was no trickery afoot. The king must have believed that without IA's backing, I could be no possible match for his fiend play and that my request to meet was no more than me on my knees begging for my life. Apparently he spoke to Peter as if he was the shit he had just stepped in.

'Thank you, shopkeeper,' he had said, contemptuously. 'You have been most useful even if you did rudely awaken me with your beckoning spell. I will let you live this time.'

One look at him made Peter shiver, yet appreciate the powerful medieval barbarous physique that was hidden under his twenty-first century garb.

He had then taken his leave.

Booby checked his watch for the umpteenth time. 'Time to go Ally. I'm ever so frightened!' I was lounging on the sofa with Lady Tam's head on my lap as I held the cold compress to her eye helping in my own sweet way to alleviate the swelling. His words were a well-timed reminder as I had just extinguished my smoke and the clock in the kitchen chimed out the eleven dings in confirmation.

'Lend us the keys to your Bentley Tams.' It sounded a reasonable rather than an ambitious request to me as I had uttered it cheekily.

By 11.45pm Booby and I were stood in the gateway of a large field high on the moor, a couple of miles out of the town. For those less learned, Lanyon's Quoit is type typical of a single-chamber megalithic tomb. It consists of three vertical megaliths and these supported a bloody big, and at over twelve tonnes, very heavy, flat, horizontal capstone. My research earlier in the day suggested that it dated from the early Neolithic times. Mathematics was always a favourite subject at school so

I had also thought-out a poor man's power to ratio calculation and at over two and a quarter ton plus full tank of gas our luxurious six litre mode of transport was going to be more than just stylish.

We were less than fifty metres away, parked just off the narrow road pointing directly at the ancient monument with the Bentley's lights blazing on main beam, illuminating the whole scene. Our arrival had purposely alarmed the few wild horses who returned to their grazing and dozing, and I stood one side of the car unburdened, other than the lighter and chalk in my pocket. Booby stood in laden contrast on the passenger side holding our now rotting Sunday joint, still in its fully thawed plastic butcher's bag and dripping blood, in one hand and with a bright red chock-full plastic petrol can in the other.

'I can't believe how you have turned her Ally! She's washed our clothes, fed us and now she's lent us her husband's magnificent car, all without question! I bet he'll be terribly annoyed if he finds out.'

'Oh, he'll find out all right Boobs. It's all down to my charm though son,' I bragged, 'Come on mate, let's get set up, we haven't got much time left before our guests arrive.'

I knew it was going to take a whole lot more than charm from this point on and I hoped my briefing to

Booby had been clear and concise enough because his participation was going to be crucial.

'Give us a bunk up pal,' I commanded, and in an instant after using Booby as a mounting block, I was atop the monument with the capstone beneath me as my temporary stage. Booby passed the bag containing our decomposing pork joint up first, followed by the petrol can and then I gave him what I hoped wouldn't be my final instructions.

'Right, you know what to do Boobs. Stay out of sight in the motor and when I give you the sign stick it in drive and floor it.'

Booby made a massive gulp in apprehension, remembering dully the part I had mapped out for him in this wild enterprise.

Now, sitting cross-legged in a mantra position, I must have looked the business. In front of me, I had unwrapped the fetid joint of pork, added a little petrol from the can and had lit it. It blazed, burning in its own fat and bled down off the side of the monument, its melting gruesome trail of blubber freefalling alight onto the grass below. On the capstone behind me, I had neatly and accurately drawn a large Celtic Broken Sun Cross in chalk. Booby was now also fully hidden under a blanket, head down inside the Bentley with its lights off. Other than the wild horses who looked a little alarmed by the slow fire dripping onto the parched ground below the capstone, we were lit by the moon and totally alone.

I had closed my eyes for fully five minutes. I didn't need a clock to tell me midnight had arrived and with it, as I reopened my peepers, I saw the king poised majestically in his medieval battle dress and armed to the teeth. Luck, don't fail me now. He wasn't alone though, at a far corner of the field stood a tall, beautiful half-woman, half-horse figure. She was, I could just make out, blue in tinge even in this dim light. Just like London buses, these deities it seemed came two by two, but of course, I was the only person fully expecting the four-legged one. I recognised her from my expansive studies earlier in the day, as Epona, the Celtic protector of horses, ponies, donkeys, and mules and I also knew that fortunately for my benefit, she protected them with particular jealousy at this specific location.

King Constantine and Epona observed each other, both tense and on guard, instantly recognising a potential adversary. The king was first to speak, raising his ball and chain which, I was beginning to appreciate, was his favourite toy. 'Why do you come here to spoil my business Centaur?'

Epona reared at the king's aggressive words, indicating the wild horses and ponies with her out-splayed front hooves, to answer in righteous anger.

'I come to protect my clan from fallacies and human threat alike Chalcedonian King!'

King Constantine turned and pointed back in fury at me as I sat all Zen-like atop the capstone.

'I will deal with you after I have shattered this Celtic myth that you have somehow summoned trickster!'

'Fill your boots big man!' was the best I could manage in witty one-liners given the circumstances.

Epona by now was seething with hatred toward the king and setting her coordinates.

'I am Genius Loci of this place, pretender, my people were here millennia before your barbaric ancestors,' and with that she began her charge.

My smile was frozen somewhere between fear and fascination. I knew the blazing pork would startle the wild horses and I also knew that their alarm would be sensed by the local 'Spirit of the Shrine' who would in turn take a cautionary butchers. I hoped that the Celtic Broken Cross I had scrawled in chalk behind me was enough to protect me from her in the short term and from him for eternity.

Her charge was accompanied by a banshee-like scream, only the king was first to strike as he avoided her trampling hooves, swinging his heavy mace from around his head and through his shoulders' projected arc. The spiked ball caught Epona full on her withers, digging deep and ripping out a huge chunk of horse-meat. The king seemed pleased that he had struck a decisive, perhaps even fatal blow, but his pleasure was short-lived as he took a vicious kick at maximum velocity to his upper torso and was badly hurt as she passed by at full pelt. I love a good scrap!

Constantine was knocked to the floor, yet he sensibly crawled inside the Quoit to protect himself, now directly beneath me, before Epona could slow herself and turn. The blood spurted alarmingly from her wound, but gathering her mojo she bravely revolved, preparing to charge again. I could see from my vantage point, which was hardly the restricted view of the cheap seats, that the king had pulled himself to his feet and was clinging to the upright closest to where the fat dripped down aflame, very near to his unprotected back. He was in a bad way, but not, unfortunately gravely wounded and he foolishly began to taunt the Centaur.

'There is not enough room for you to breach me in here, witch. I shall watch you haemorrhage your life-force and then it will be my pleasure to dispose of the human filth who forced our conflict!'

That was all the bad mouthing I could take, so without any sort of dignified pause, I emptied the contents of the petrol can down onto the king's shoulders. The blazing fat adjacent ignited his frame fully and he staggered inside the Quoit lit up like a firework screaming in agony trying to roll the flames out on the ground. Standing fully upright, I waved my arms toward the Bentley and seeing the forgotten Booby's sweaty and petrified face illuminated by the king's combustion, he was now poised and ready behind the steering wheel. I screamed the instruction, 'Now! Give it the gun Boobs!' Without further ceremony or invite, the Bentley accelerated hard across the field building critical speed as it went and crashed impressively headlong into the front upright stone that was supporting the roof of the Quoit that I was presently leaping from as if my life depended on it, which of course it did. The Bentley's airbags deployed and swallowed Booby whole, while I rolled like a paratrooper as I hit the deck, landing in a foreign field under enemy fire, all just in time to see twelve tonnes of dislodged capstone fall on top of the burning monarch. Game, set and match to me I believed!

'Well done mate!' I exclaimed gratefully as I pulled the stricken Booby from the wrecked dream machine, also glancing around nervously to note that Epona was gone, her enemy now destroyed. The capstone with its covering Celtic Broken Sun Cross symbol made the perfect headstone and a fitting resting place for the feudal despot so, lighting a much desired cigarette in tribute, I offered a few concluding words of committal as the wild horses returned to their grazing, 'rest in peace arsehole!'

Booby had slumped to the grass all shell-shocked and unnecessary, so after helping him back to his feet as sympathetically as I could, we made our way, with me in the supporting role, past the impaled Bentley, which was leaking fluid all over the shop and steaming like a boiling kettle.

'Come on mate, we better split the scene, I don't think even I could explain this little lot away!'

Part Five

The Black Manilishi

The granite wall was as hard as, well granite I suppose, as the two of us sat uncomfortably upon it at the end of Smeaton's Pier. The midday sun was strong as we had now moved into summertime proper and my undesirable companion perched beside me, moaning his tits off.

'Thirty-seven grand the damage to my Bentley will cost to repair Mr Crowley,' explained the fat, pretentious Lord Terrance Trivago.

'I'm sure it won't come out of your pocket, mush,' I replied spitefully.

The lord rocked back on his oversized buttocks and stubbed his cigar out under his shiny black loafers as he laughingly agreed, 'no, of course not, that's what the taxpayers are for after all.'

I could sense him scrutinising me with his piggy little eyes as he continued to speak.

'I underestimated you, Mr Crowley and I am here to offer my sincere apologies and hopefully come to some sort of amicable agreement?'

That was big of the malicious fucker, especially as he had just tried to have me killed, setting his medieval madman the task on his behalf. There was only ever going to be one offer from me in response. 'You stop trying to kill me and lay off your wife you fat bastard and I'll leave you alone. How's that grab you porky?' And with that I walked away feeling his eyes boring into my back. I never trust a man with a grudge, but at least he knew exactly where he stood.

At the end of the pier there was a squadron of cats, the Black Manilishi at their head with the obvious intention of offering me a guided escort. It was an invitation I knew better than to refuse so rather than go and have a gander at the clean-up operation that had been ongoing back at the studio apartment for more than a week now, I veered left and followed the moggies along the quayside. It wasn't hard to work out where we were going.

Entering the parish church, I witnessed the cats, minus the Black Manilishi, disperse, while the aforementioned sat down by the font and returned to his favourite hobby of licking his balls. The view wasn't a pleasant one, neither were the frozen figures of the trapped personalities of Phillip Browne and Richard Soul encased in concrete on the side of the font replacing the customary angels. This all served to remind me of the power that was sitting halfway down the aisle dressed in twenty-first century Boho-chic and backpack.

Positioning myself politely in a pew adjacent to the saint, I bowed my head more in good manners than reverence and began, 'I haven't prayed for years IA, but don't suppose you have summoned me here to say one now though, have you?'

She never even moved her head to look at me, then answered a little too honestly and without comfort for my liking. 'No magician, your soul is beyond simple prayer I am afraid.'

Stoically, I settled, 'That's good to know, so we won't be dealing with any blackmail or suchlike then?'

IA now turned toward me calmly as she continued our dialogue. 'No blackmail or deception on my part you can be assured. Today I speak on behalf of one who has helped in no small way to safeguard you, thus far.'

She had laboured the, 'Thus far' bit to make a point and at the same instant she pointed toward the Black Manilishi who in turn, gave an appreciative Meeeeeeeeeeeeeeeow.

'Let me paint you a picture Mr Crowley.' She continued and moved her fingers through the air like a fantasy paintbrush. I am not sure if the image that appeared was really there or if she had indeed placed it within my mind, but it was as clear as day for only me to see.

'He was not always a simple cat, Mr Crowley. The tale I shall tell and magically illustrate inside your mind will help to explain our next engagement.' With that, my inner vision opened with a scene of the working harbour of St Ives, over two hundred years before. The main subject of my revelation was a finely dressed, handsome young man eating an apple, whilst all around him were hectic fishermen, their wives and children all busily packing pilchards into the salting barrels, preparing for what was evidently, a very lucrative marketplace.

'This was the year of our lord 1796 Mr Crowley, a record year for the catch.' She paused as the young man spat the pips from his fruit onto the ground with contemptuous disregard for the workers struggling around him. His act made it clear to all about, that for him, hard work was not on the agenda.

'You are observing young Mr William Nancarrow and he has recently returned to St Ives after the best education money could buy at Oxford University.' My mental background scene faded and changed now to the inside of a large manor house and William being spoken to by those whom I rightly assumed were his well-to-do parents.

'You can see that William's mother and father are pleading with their feckless son and regardless of the import of their topic, he looks wholly disinterested. By now I was fascinated, 'His enriched family have high hopes that William will join the family shipping business. Alas, he has more pleasurable endeavours in mind.'

Again, the sight shifted, this time to a tavern where the callow youth was drinking and whoring as if he was in a Hogarth's Gin Lane cartoon of a previous generation. The panorama changed quickly as if embarrassed and this time no words were necessary: William's father's pointing arm as he slings his son out of the family home and behind her husband, William's mother distraughtly weeping.

IA paused shortly then continued her story, 'His father could not tolerate the exposed un-godliness of it all and cast his spawn adrift of the household and as a natural consequence, its fortune.'

My next historic view focused on the yet again drunken William, now sat alone back at the tavern. This time, however the landlord was glaring at him behind his back.

'One thing to live the Bohemian existence Mr Crowley, quite another thing to be able to pay for it,'

With the saint's wise words I witnessed the landlord toss the drunken William out on his ear. He landed without dignity, heavily on the sodden cobbles outside. Rising up slowly, he gathered what he could of his muddled senses and then staggered off while the entire crowd, who he had previously held in such low esteem, laughed and spat mercilessly at him.

'Down on his luck, only blazing with sinful pride his education was however not wasted.'

William's life story continued and now he was sitting on a large rock on the beach, sobering up in the vicious rain and looking bitterly out to sea for inspiration, no doubt.

'Soaked through, he walks back along the harbour road, all the time hatefully looking at the old, bent, overworked fisher folk he despises for their poverty. He needs a business venture to supply him with the means for a lifestyle he unjustly thinks he deserves. An artless, timeless business calculation occurs to him. Buy cheap, sell high. Better still if he could steal.'

The heavens opened harder and William was next seen sheltering in the Market House doorway as a funeral procession passed by and on through the parish church lychgate. A priest led the way at the head of the grieving family, onward into the churchyard and the committal.

The saint's story was as unremitting as the rain.

'A successful business venture is conceived in William's sharp mind. This is the age of, 'Resurrectionism' Mr Crowley, and dead bodies are just the low-cost commodity he is looking for. He is soon to embark on his new career as a grave robber, a body snatcher. To him it is just simple supply and demand.'

The view now changed location and panned out beyond the green lawns in front the Royal Devon and Exeter Hospital, identified by its extensive signage. Doctors and students were busily hurrying about their business.

'This establishment is famous as a teaching hospital and the rewards are more than ample, with top premiums paid and no questions asked, for quality fresh cadavers. However, the penalty for detection is greater.'

With that observation the sight of the gallows at Exeter Gaol flashed into view.

This storyboard was all coming together unpleasantly enough, and just to make sure that I got the gist and didn't drift off the Black Manilishi bared his diamond white fangs at me and hissed. IA seemed annoyed that her story had been interrupted by her feline assistant ahead of her reveal yet she carried on regardless.

'Back to my tale trickster.' The image returned to St Ives, with two scruffs with wooden shovels at the head of a fresh grave whilst a third man, William, plays look-out, holding a lantern that emits just enough light to work by, but not enough to raise alarm.

'It does not take William long to find men willing to do the dirty work,'

The view was now of Fore Street where he was striding about in all his finery, oblivious to the jealous stares he was attracting and the comments his detractors were making.

'Jealously and suspicion make powerful bedfellows and it wasn't long before his enterprise was exposed.'

The saint's words were true for any time and place.

William's two assistants are now seen drunk and bragging in a local alehouse while another sneaky looking individual sits close by, overhearing their gusto. Next, the sneaky man moves to a darkened corner of the barroom and is observed whispering into the ear of a seated, portly looking gentleman, apparently of some standing and import, who in return, slips a bag of coins beneath the table to his apparent informant. 'It wasn't long before the message of doom was enthusiastically deployed,' sighed the saint.

Before she had even finished her last sentence, the scene had shifted to a court house.

Just as a judge, complete with black cap passes the death sentence and slams the gavel down hard on the block, the three defendants shuffle in their chains, the two earth movers are in rags while William stands defiant, still the dandy. His father, seen in the background, can only lean upon the backrest in front of him, severely shocked, while William's poor mother weeps again, uncontrollably. The sneaky man, alongside his portly gentleman employer, looks pleased with their enterprise. The rest of the crowd, who are packed in all around the condemned men, cheer happily at the condemnation. An aural conclusion fills the air as the Judge finishes his work for the day. 'And may the Lord have mercy on your souls. Take them away!'

I wasn't expecting an interlude, but IA left a short gap for the sake of decency before her tale and the vision restarted. Some little time has apparently passed and with all hope of reprieve faded, William looks nearly as ragged as his two accomplices, featured in their filthy cell at a point just before they are about to be dragged to the cart waiting outside to take them to the scaffold. William is on his knees praying hard.

Soon at the gallows the three now stand side by side before a huge, excited crowd, their necks already in their greasy nooses and now, accompanied by a great cheer, the trap is sprung and they drop, somehow surprised, to their doom.

My implanted vision was now gone completely, and IA took centre stage in my consciousness once again.

'Although his crimes were abhorrent, I heard his prayer and luckily had a use for his soul. His life became my gift, so the day William Nancarrow's humanity left his body at the end of the rope, I made him my animal servant.'

She looked over at the large, black tom taking my eyes with her and concluded her tale.

'The Black Manilishi was born, fully formed and in all his majesty!'

The cat sat resplendently still by the font. Buoyed up no doubt by his longwinded yet excitingly tragic introduction, on the face of it he looked contented to be the centre of attention now his origin had been fully explained. It wasn't the type of tale you could enjoy, I know, but considering it was coming from the mouth of a saint, I knew it to be true.

'So, you transferred William's spirit into a local moggy at the point of his death. He must have been thrilled!'

Taking out my packet of Super Kings and leaning casually on the font, the two trapped retailers came into sight again in their prison carvings.

'He was relieved rather than thrilled Mr Crowley, and he has remained so for over two hundred years, always at my beck and call.'

It wasn't hard to know where all this was going, so I thought I would impress her up front with my powers of perception. 'Don't tell me darlin, now he has paid his dues and you want to reincarnate him?' And then pointing at the two figures cast upon the font, 'and don't tell me, let them two jokers out as well, I dare say?' Flipping my lighter top and igniting my cigarette I concluded, 'just one problem, then, you need a replacement body!'

IA turned away and looked upward at her own stained glass image and I couldn't help but feel pleased when she said, 'You display remarkable insight, magician.'

'You need to in this game luv,' it was a simple statement of fact backed up by my years of hard won experience, rather than a cocky aside.

There were only a few shoppers milling around the eclectic retailers upon the Market Square, so without distraction, my thoughts turned to my pious challenge. I needed to find a suitable host for an ex-body snatcher who was now stuck inside a cat! Not just any cat, but the so-called Black Manilishi, and I was more than gratefully aware of this animal's contribution toward my safe keeping. If it hadn't have been for him, I would have been pushing up the daisies weeks before. Also, there was a need to tie all this in with the reintroduction of the two soul-caged idiot shopkeepers and that was going to take some hell of a diversion spell. It was all going to be easy peasy then!

Approaching the studio down the inclining backroad, it was pleasing to see that most of the devastation caused by the recent Atlantic Ocean incursion was recovering to something near normal. There were numerous workmen along with property owners, shifting sand and effecting the repairs and refurbishments necessary. Booby had appointed himself as some sort of unofficial foreman and was effeminately bossing and bitching a couple of scruffs about and they were unsurprisingly, looking none too pleased about it all.

'Come on men, chop, chop! We want to get back in tonight, not next Christmas you know.'

The two workmen hadn't seen me approaching and the first one bad-temperedly bit him back, 'You ain't liftin' much are you Shirley?'

He was quickly joined by his supportive workmate, 'Not unless you count his shirt-tail Sid, hah, hah, hah!'

My arm was around this second comedian's shoulder in a flash and I pulled him close, smelling the rank combination of sweat, coffee, piss and I like to think a little fear, as I offered him some much needed and timely advice, all dressed up in a friendly warning. 'That's not very funny my old son. It's a dangerous place a worksite like this and we wouldn't want you having a little accident now, would we?' He seemed to get the message and along with his newly apprehensive looking pal, he re-energised his efforts so the possibility of our return that night was looking more probable by the minute.

Booby had marched, seemingly infuriated with my intervention, into the apartment and following in after him, I was further impressed to see the place clean and devoid of sand. 'You didn't have to speak up for me Ally, I can cope with the riff-raff you know!'

'I know you can Boobs,' I replied, trying to reassure him. 'You shouldn't need to though, should you?' Soon we were both humping and lumping away in silence, bringing in new furniture and fittings and our recent hiccup was forgotten.

I never was one for manual work so after I had slipped out for a crafty drag, leaving Booby to add some finishing touches, I thought it might be a good idea to go and see how the soon-to-be-divorced Lady Muck was. Approaching Norway Square, I was surprised to see Tamsin sitting melancholy in this tranquil area amongst the flowers. Her shiner had faded considerably, and the swelling gone down so her aristocratic, high cheek boned looks had returned. Standing aside, I offered her one of my Super K's and without thanks, she tearfully shared her concerns.

'He's started proceedings Alex, my name will be mud.'

That was hard to refute, so I held her hands, pulling her to her feet and tried to cheer her up. 'Don't worry darlin', he'll keep his beak shut if he knows what's good for him. Come on, let's go and have a bevvy.'

The Sloop was packed and as we squeezed in through the doorway a rather snooty looking middle-aged, middle class, dumpy looking woman screwed her face up in disgust at Tamsin. This was the sort who previously, I dare say, couldn't do enough to be acquainted with Her Ladyship, so I again found myself offering some well-placed, but uninvited advice.

'If the wind changes you'll stick like that you old cow!'

Sitting in the pub's famous round room, our neighbours on the next table seemed less bothered by our presence and after a few G&T's, Lady T began to relax a little. It was time to make my offer, 'Look, we'll be back in the studio tonight, come and stay with me and Boobs until this all blows over.'

She seemed shocked at my proposal, 'A… ar… are you sure?'

I wasn't asking her to marry me. We both laughed, realising the absurdity of our reactions considering all that had recently happened.

'Of course, I'm sure,' I confirmed, 'just returning the favour luv, after all.'

Well past midnight and I lay wide awake in the new king size double. Tamsin was spark out beside me and through the open door, I concentrated on the dozing figure of Booby, sat slumped in an armchair with a book balanced on his lap. It's funny how the best ideas arrive just when you are not expecting them or in my case even deserving of them. As I focused intently on Booby's dribbling face I thought about what Lucky Lucian had told me about him. It seemed he had the big disease with a little name and the prognosis was not good. As I entertained myself, childishly blowing smoke rings, I weighed up all the options, apparently, he only had a few years to live at best so I decided there and then that with regard to Booby, IA, the two shopkeepers and in particular, The Black Manilishi, I was going to do them all a massive favour, whether they liked it or not!

They say two's company but three's a crowd and I for one can vouch for that!

As Lady T and I sat eating breakfast in peace, Booby fluttered around the kitchen in a style that I can only describe as irritating. Her Ladyship's nerves were beginning to fray as my well-intentioned housemate approached her from the side and decanted a large, obscenely shaped sausage onto her plate using his thumb to liberate it from the reluctant prongs.

'You always did like a nice bit of pork first thing in the morning, didn't you ducky?' he said sarcastically as the sausage skidded in its own grease across her platter.

Tamsin looked up slowly at her disrespectful waiter, and with contempt written as a fine veneer across her tense face retorted, 'I hope you have washed your hands de Faux!'

It wasn't really meant as a question more of an insult and Booby quickly returned fire, 'I hope you've cleaned your teeth!'

Her ladyship sprang upward toward him and her dinner knife was at Booby's throat before he could adjust his indignant stance and remove his hand from his hip. Thankfully for him, I managed to get between them like a referee in a boxing match as I am sure she would have split him from arse to head on the spot!

'Easy girls!' I attempted to diffuse the situation and Booby took the time out to walk away shakily, while the aristocrat drove her dinner knife hard into the table top as a sort of compensatory reward. Blue bloods could be so entertaining, only I must admit I preferred mine red, or better still, not at all.

Booby hadn't got a good word to say about Tamsin all day and he took another opportunity to show his disapproval later that evening as we headed out of town in a classic vintage yellow VW Beetle, circa 1961. 'I didn't think she looked too keen on lending you this old wreck Ally.'

'Well, after what happened to her husband's Bentley it's hardly surprising is it mate?' I countered, before entering my plea, 'I wish you would stop sniping at her though Boobs. It's causing me stress and strain.'

He looked incredulous at my suggestion and snapped, 'It's her Ally! I think she's jealous!'

At that, I really needed to put him back in his box, 'Oh, I'm sure the tall, thin, rich, sophisticated and beautifully manicured Lady T is green with envy when she looks at you mate.'

If I thought that was game over I was wrong, it seems my box wasn't bitch proof and he continued to leak his venom heedlessly, 'She's vicious! I thought she was going to stick that knife into my throat.'

'You were asking for it mate,' I confirmed unsympathetically as I floored the pedal, forcing Hitler's favourite model struggling up the hill and although I knew full well this machine was performing to its classic best, it really couldn't pull the skin off a rice pudding.

Three quarters of an hour later, what was left of the daylight had disappeared along with any trace of humanity as we parked the Beetle on a dehydrated and rutted grass verge. Bodmin Moor was a hilly, barren landscape. Eighty square desolate miles of granite moorland. A few cows and wild horses spotted around and even fewer trees. The odd mysterious dark pool added to the ambience and it was a great place for a murder. Looking over from our current vantage point, I daren't let Booby know we were going to the highest place in Cornwall known as 'Brown Willy' as he might have got the wrong idea!

Ahead on the horizon stood the rudely named highpoint, which had got the blame for all sorts of unlikely natural phenomena over the years as well as providing the rustic refuge and concealment for the beast that I was intending to re-acquaint myself with this very night. Next to the layby's 'No Tipping' sign, screwed insecurely to the rotting wooden stile that gave entry to the land beyond, were an old television, sofa and fridge, reminding me that indeed modern-day mischief could in fact, live side by side with ancient menace.

Without ceremony I gave the marching orders, 'Come on Boobs, shake a leg. We've got a bit of a ramble ahead of us I reckon.'

'Why are we here Ally? It all looks a little lonely,' he queried.

'Gotta see a man about a dog mate. Well, a cat to be more precise,' came my cryptic answer and with that we were over the gateway and on our way.

With Booby trailing behind, mopping his brow often and over-demonstratively for my benefit, with his pink spotted handkerchief, silently demonstrating the efforts he was making, I remembered the last time I had encountered the rogue I was now seeking. It had been a long time, but I'd had my suspicions as to his whereabouts for a number of years, yet as he wasn't causing me any grief personally, I had decided to give him the swerve. Until now of course.

The moon was high enough to illuminate a landscape that mirrored its own, and there atop the promontory rocks of the Tor stood a large brown puma with three smaller versions attendant within spitting distance. I was right, I knew the bastard was here. I should have cleaned up the mess I made last time we fought, but I was in a bad way myself after our little tiff and it was all I could do back then to crawl away from the wreckage.

We were close enough now to be heard. Booby was amazed and frightened, not only by the sight of the large cat, but also because I expected a reply to the question I now posed it, 'How about you come down here old son so we can have a chin-wag?' I suggested.

Booby turned to look questioningly at me. 'If it replies, I'll just die!'

It did better than that as it stood on its hind legs and effortlessly morphed into human shape. 'Booby, let me introduce you to Mr De Havilland,' seemed a natural enough introduction to me, although it was wasted as my effeminate friend had fainted away face first with an, 'oh my God!'

De Havilland was fairly typical of his breed, a long streak of piss and with an unnerving whiteness to his skin. His sunken cheeks emphasised the stare that he placed me under, as he trawled through his memory to figure out who I was. Pleasingly, I couldn't have changed too much with age, as I had only just left my teens the last time I saw him and it didn't take him long to identify me, as after all, it was down to me that he had ended up in this unhappy predicament, abandoned on the moors.

'How did you know I was here Crowley?'

These were probably the first words he had uttered to a human being for over twenty years. It was nice to see that he had enough respect and fear of me to stay rooted to the spot, dressed in a sort of black jumpsuit get-up which made him look like a cross between David Bowie and Elvis Presley. His long, thin limbs didn't give much of an impression of the muscle or the physical power he possessed, although I knew better than to get too close or within striking distance myself as we continued our re-acquaintance.

'Call it instinct old son. I like to keep an eye out for any unusual occurrences.'

With that insight I nonchalantly lifted my left foot up onto the rock in front of me, dropped my elbow to my knee and lit a cigarette in a sort of long, slow movement ending with a stance that I was hoping showed me off in all my arrogant confidence. It was of course bravado rather than self-assurance, it was logical to me that there was obviously something preventing the vampire from attacking there and then and more to the point, keeping him here, isolated in this wilderness.

'I didn't think all the drained sheep and horses were down to just a big rogue kitty cat, it was bound to be more Mary Shelley than Mary Chipperfield wasn't it?'

De Havilland gave a little chuckle at that, which unpleasantly exposed his yellow fangs. I was glad I couldn't smell his breath from that distance, and I glared deeply into his eyes and pointed at the three female pumas standing aggressively at his side.

'Seems you got married, then mate? Not sure if that is bestiality or bigamy!'

De Havilland motioned to his harem, and they relaxed instantly. 'You always were a cocky fucker Crowley.'

'Too fly for you Dracula!' He always hated that reference and winced as I moved to the front of the rock to sit upon it, noting that Booby was still spark out.

'I have a mutually advantageous offer to make to you, vampire. I wouldn't think your feline existence hereabouts is very satisfactory, I am sure you much preferred your bat in the belfry, huh?'

I stubbed my cigarette out and indicated my unconscious housemate without looking directly at his prone body, keeping the vampire in view at all times.

'You need human blood I assume to regather your previous strength and I need a body drained of it. My friend here needs no more than a chance to survive. A win, win situation, so to speak.'

Ten minutes later, after we had discussed the details of our suggested alliance, I helped the recovering Booby to his feet, brushing the dirt from his nose and walked warily away from the encounter. Once Booby was upright, I looked toward the summit rocks, De Havilland had reverted to his feline state and wandered back into his cover, his three wives in close attendance, loyally protecting his rear.

The trek down helped to bring Booby back to his senses. He was sorely relieved to get inside the Beetle, intent on taking the driver's seat and to getting us as far away from the moor as was possible. At least him driving gave me a chance to mull over what I had just learned and put everything into some sort of context that made sense. I knew the 'Beast of Bodmin' was just a cover and the dates of activity lined up conveniently with our last encounter. De Havilland had been up on the moor for over twenty years, at first just the dust and bone that I hadn't cleaned up, as I was in too bad a state following our previous fight on Plymouth Hoe. He had made the classic vampire mistake of attacking me too late in the night and was hideously exposed as the dawn broke and as I further delayed him, struggling for my life alongside Smeaton's Tower. I had been more than relieved at that time to see De Havilland revert to a pile of smouldering skeletal ash and bone. However, I was too young and inexperienced in my unchosen occultist career, and unable to understand what I needed to do next. I had fled the scene before I could be caught by the police who were closing in fast and had become more of a priority.

I squinted as my cigarette smoke wafted into my eyes and continued to reconstruct the rest of the events that De Havilland had filled me in with. It seemed a seagull had picked De Havilland's jawbone from the burning mound and after lugging it sky bound many a mile, decided that the weight wasn't worth the effort and dropped it like a stone at the edge of the moor. Seems that one of the three original pumas that were loose at the time, thanks to Mary C, had chewed on matey boy's mandible and there was enough marrow left in it to infect the poor buggar with the vampiric blasphemy.

The bump in the road shocked me from my thoughts as the Beetle took off, with all four wheels liberated from terra firma due to the excessive speed Booby had coaxed out of the old jalopy in his urge to return to the town. 'Steady on Boobs!' I cried, 'you trying to get us killed? That's my job mate!'

Returning to my thoughts I put two and two together and concluded the rest of the origin of the species' story that I had rationally pieced together in my head. After a bit of the natural feline hanky panky, a new over-sized alfa male cub had been born in a litter of six and took its natural place in the pecking order as the half dozen grew up together. A vampire literally reborn and with the natural fangs to die for into the bargain no less!

De Havilland knew that I had worked out that for some reason he was trapped on the moor and it was sensible for him to fess up the real reason, knowing all too well that my suggested deal was in the offing. Because of his unnatural rebirth he had inherited a little too much moggy DNA and that was enough to ensure the part of him that appeared in his humanlike form was only sustainable for around fifteen frustrating minutes. He also hadn't got the strength to overcome any human prey to fill up his tank, so my suggestion of a willing donor seemed just the ticket. The fact that Booby's blood was tainted was of no concern to him other than he didn't care for the taste overmuch, having sampled it on previous occasions back in his heyday. It was only a Coke versus Pepsi dilemma for him!

We parked the Beetle on the slipway outside of the Sloop and were soon inside and on our second round amongst the happy and, as it was near closing time, extremely pissed clientele. Booby had bought his snifters en masse and while I was still on my first pint he had three empty glasses in front of him and was bolting down his fourth G&T. 'Oh! I needed that Ally, my nerves are shattered.' I had outlined most but not all of my plan to him. I sat back against the cushioned wall seat and in a sincere fatherly way tried to comfort him. 'I know it's hard for you Boobs, you're going to have to trust me on this one big time I am afraid.'

His imploring face looked innocently at me and he spoke in a sheepish and discreet manner, 'I do trust you Ally, h … how did you know about my errr, little problem?'

Leaning forward to make sure he retained his confidence and his dignity, I gave him the facts. 'Lucian's got a big mouth mate, plus it was probably him that infected you in the first place.'

At this point he was close to tears but managed to sob stutter, 'I…I…I loved him Ally and he just used me.'

I placed my fist playfully under his chin and offered a pick me up.

'Old story I'm afraid Boobs. Come on now, pull your head off the floor. Come up screaming!'

With our spirits lifted and in our now rather over-refreshed state we soon made for home, with the now merry funster Booby de Faux Esquire rendering his version of John Denver's, 'Country Roads' as he careered precariously along the narrow side streets behind the wheel of the pristine yellow VW, until he got to the bit about, 'To the place where I belong,' which unfortunately turned out to be the hard granite steps on the side of a roadside cottage. As the Beetle's irresistible momentum carried it across the unmovable object, it left its driver's side front wing along with the front bumper in its guilty wake. The noisy smashing and scraping of metal on stonework had alerted the holidaymakers inside. I am sure they only caught a glimpse of this masterpiece of German engineering, disappearing into the distance using both sides of the roadside like a pinball against the cushions.

Derek and Joan Panalba were truly the salt of the earth and the following day they attended an unexpected appointment having been summoned by none other than Lord Terrance Trivago himself, at his posh sea front hotel that also bore his family name. His Lordship sat cross-legged reading the St Ives Times and Echo while Derek and Joan sipped their tea politely. The periodicals front page proudly blazed the headline 'Midsummer, St Ives Biathlon is GO, GO, GO!'

Lord Terrance sat the paper down on the coffee table and began the conversation, 'It is great news indeed, Mr and Mrs Panalba is it not?'

'Oh, please calls us Derek and Joan Mr Errm?' responded the sweet old lady.

'Lord Terrance or Sir will be fine my dear,' replied the self-important tosser, before continuing unfazed, 'We will be counting on your support errr, Derek and Joan, along with all our other splendid volunteers to make a resounding success out of this year's race, even after all the unseemly disorder we have recently suffered.' He made an affected effort to stand before walking over to the large picture window which overlooked the harbour in all its glory. Turning back, he looked snidely down upon his seated guests.

'It has been a bit of a rum year all round I am sorry to say and the boost that the Biathlon will bring to my … errr, the local economy shall be most welcome.'

That must have tugged at Joan's heart strings as naively, she rallied.

'We'll all do our bests Your Lordship, you can counts on us. Is late notice, but we has a week at least to get all shipshape and Bristol fashion.'

With that Lord Terrance threw open his arms in faux support and spat out, 'That's the spirit, my woman! If there is anything I can do to help, morally of course, please do not hesitate to ask my secretary.'

Their teacups were still half full yet they were shown out of Hotel Trivago's grand entrance before the lord's insincerities had even stopped resonating. The doorman, all top hat and tails behind them, clapped his hands together to remove any trace of the pensioners from his white gloves as if they were the scum of the earth and they trotted off suitably invigorated and inspired along the cobbled road with Derek chattering, 'We has better get a leg on girl, we gots lots to do.'

Then Joan joined in, 'I wonder if that nice Mr Crowley would give us an 'and? Seeing's as it was him that roped in ol Lord Snooty Pants after all.'

It seemed they weren't as stupid as His Lordship had imagined and they carried on snickering as they walked away.

On the patio outside the Coast Watch Station at a small round table complete with quaint floral tablecloth, Derek and Joan told the story of their meeting with Lord Terrance as Lady Tamsin and I sat listening, amused. Their efforts were both entertaining and to plan. Joan leaned over my shoulder with a huge teapot and poured accurately, 'One lump or two Mr Crowley?'

It was a stock answer, but I couldn't help myself, 'Only one luv, I'm sweet enough!'

Devotedly, Derek took over the conversation, 'So's we can count on your support then, thas' great. We only have as week till Sat'day tea time to pull this one off. Is a big ask.'

Lady Tamsin's face was a treat as I seized the moment, 'No sweat Dek's. Lady T will whip up the Women's Institute and the Roundtable, Boobs will harness his biking pals and I'll gather up the waifs and strays. A week is plenty.' It was a bold statement.

As we walked away, arm in arm down the steep grassy slope from the station, Tamsin meekly complained, 'Thanks for volunteering me Alex,' to which I chirped back, 'my pleasure darlin'.

The call to arms went out forthwith and it cheered my old cockles to see that all and sundry came to the assist. Over the next week bunting went up all over the shop, hot cakes sold like, well, hot cakes, road directions were sorted, leaflets were printed and distributed, all in preparation for the one event left that summer that could save the season. I was more than proud to be a part of it, notwithstanding the fact that if it hadn't been for my presence, the malady that had overtaken the town would never have happened in the first place.

I also had other business to attend to, so later that day, once I had delegated good works around my new-found friends, I made my way to the Market Place where the recent building works were neatly and nearly concluded. It's always fair to say that any geezer dressed in hard hat, overalls and builder's safety boots is permanently up for earning a few bob extra, so I beckoned over a likely-looking lad.

'Oi mush! Can I have a word in your shell-like?'

After a little chat and a few quid up front, I patted the preliminary wad into his top pocket and he confirmed his assistance, 'Right mate, no bother, oil have that done for you by Sat'day teatime.'

'It's a date then pal, Saturday, 8.45pm, The Guildhall. Don't be late, be lucky.'

The week passed by in a whirl of hard work and comradeship, something that I had never before witnessed to any great degree and as the race horizon shortened all the arranging and doing was completed without hiccup. All was pleasant enough back at the studio as Booby tried his best with Lady Tamsin, but I was aware even then, of the gulf in class between us.

The sun hadn't quite appeared yet on the Saturday morning horizon as I stood peering and trying to cut through the darkness using Booby's costly binoculars from the studio apartment's French doors. Less than a mile away, up on the headland that lay parallel with the Island but was separated from it by the long stretch of Porthmeor Beach, stood an old rundown building that I guessed dated back to the Second World War and probably was used then, as some sort of defence post or look out. This headland along with the rest of the beach and foreshore had been marked as, 'Out of Bounds' following the shark attack. The ugly restriction of the barricades was very much in vogue. The metal petals of the razor wire shimmered softly, reflected by a sea that was calm on a tide that was completely in, lapping gently on the beach, only it was the movement upon the promontory that had caught my attention and even in this dull light, assisted by the eyeglasses' magnification, I could clearly make out the shapes of three large cats. The big hand on my watch said six and the little one pointed towards the four, which in my reckoning added up to two things: it was very nearly dawn on midsummer's day and also time that I paid a visit to the thin white bloodsucker.

Walking towards the building ten minutes later, wrapped snugly in my trench coat, I reasoned that I had been right to think he couldn't fly and was indeed trapped in his feline form other than for the brief fifteen-minute spells he had confessed to the last time we spoke. Once I was within twenty five yards or so of the concrete construction's open entrance, the three pumas appeared. The nearest of the three bared her fangs as a warning for me to come no closer, so I knew her master was inside, amidst the shadows. I presumed that a soothing word might be in order. 'Only me tiddles,' I taunted, 'I'm here to see your husband, brother, lover, whatever he is!' Looking past the defender, I continued to speak to the darkness beyond. 'That is you in there I take it and not the big bad wolf?'

It was the whites of his eyes that pierced the gloom first, with their blood red pupils, then I perceived the outline of the tall, thin sinister figure as he spoke in response to my disrespectful enquiry, 'You pick your time wisely conjurer as I need to retire after my exhausting four-legged journey and before the cursed sunrise, so please get to the point.'

While he made his maiden speech I lit my first tombstone of the day and now I flicked my burning match at the closest cat who took my bravado as its prompt to back off slightly. 'Straight to business it is then my old pal. Be at the Guildhall at ten tonight on the dot. It will be dark enough by then for you to manoeuvre, so meet me on the stage and we can do the exchange.'

It all seemed a simple enough instruction to me, though it was clear that he did not trust my intentions fully as he warned, 'Do not cross me Crowley. I need that human blood, even if it is tainted, to free myself of this feline restrictive.'

Taking that as a warning rather than as good advice I pulled my collar up around my lower face and assumed the pose of a 1920s Hollywood Vampire, Bela Lugosi style and comically affected an Eastern European accent, 'Don't worry mush! You'll soon be back to being a kosher member of the undead meathead brigade!'

With that, he stepped into the lightening dawn and although he must have felt the burn he continued to make his point, 'I cannot believe you will be pleased that I shall roam unshackled again, free from the restrictions of my rebirth?'

Regaining a more dignified pose I replied in all honesty for a change.

'Kitty cat or badass bat, I'm not exactly chuffed either way mate, but if your freedom to roam is the price I have to pay for my good friend's life and soul, then so be it. Ta, ta, till tonight old bean.'

I looked back once one my way back to witness the three cats entering the ruins, preparing to rest and keep their master safe as the sun started to rise above the town, highlighting the white ramparts of the Tate Gallery in its early morning glimmer.

Smeaton's Pier and yet again I sat at what had become my favourite resting spot, drinking the welcome cup of rosy that I had blagged on my way past Maggie T's. Thankfully, it wasn't the ostentatious lord sat beside me now, instead the much more pleasant company of IA, her tiny girlish figure resplendent in her Doc Martens, leggings, linen jacket and the ever-present backpack. 'Your preparations proceed well magician?'

It was nice of her to give me the credit, yet I had to put her right. 'I'm no magician darlin', I just know a few tricks is all.'

She knew the answer before she even asked her next question. 'Tricks or not, we will reorder our environs tonight?'

'That's one way of putting it, I suppose, don't worry though, it's all in hand. Be ready tonight as the light begins to fade and your bell rings nine times.'

As we looked across the harbour towards St EIA's, the two trapped images of Phillip Browne and Richard Soul lifeless on the side of the church font flashed across my mind. I wasn't surprised when IA referred to them at that very moment herself. 'My guests are purged of their evil interlopers and are cleansed ready to re-join our community, Mr Crowley.'

I was pleased for them both and made it plain to the saint.

'Good oh. I hope they have learned a little humility and some manners plus a little sense of humour along the way as I have the perfect diversion spell in mind to free them.'

She didn't want to dig deeper thankfully, so I walked away without another word, finishing my cuppa on the hop. I lit a fresh cigarette, pleased that no matter how unlikely, it seemed, she trusted me completely.

From my voyeur's paradise on the harbour wall, I watched as a multitude of holidaymakers walked about under the colourful bunting and signs that were all now in place to promote the forthcoming race. It was set fair to be the best attended and thus financially supported event of the year and I felt a sense of pride in my fellow man at the efforts that had been made to make a success of the occasion. It was only I who understood the magnitude of what was to come. Oh yes, it was going to be one hell of a spectacle alright and with that thought hanging, I returned my cup to the café and the ever-lovely Maggie, and then it was back to the studio, where my next appointment waited.

The apartment really was pristine. The flood waters had, it seemed washed all the corruption and bad vibes away at the same time as it had removed most of furniture. In their replacement I had taken the opportunity to organise and modernise and the place looked every bit twenty-first century Boho boutique. Sitting cross-legged in one of the two new leather armchairs was Lord Terrance. His legs were crossed, not in relaxation it seemed, more in protection as Lady Tamsin moved towards him joltingly with a red hot cup of coffee in her hand. Taking a pew opposite, on the new chaise lounge, likewise enjoying their hot drinks were Derek and Joan Panalba, while Booby had decided to stay busying himself in the kitchen area, seemingly concerned it could all kick off between Lord and Lady Muck.

Lord Terrance was, irritatingly, first to speak following my late entry.

'I have been waiting some little time Mr Crowley.'

I kept my cool and acknowledged him with the customary disrespect due.

'Keep your knickers on Tez. I'm sure your good lady has looked after you well.'

Tamsin was staring daggers at her estranged husband, but turned smartly on her not insubstantial heels to re-join Booby at the sink and collect her own beverage.

I sat down opposite His Lordship in the twin chair and straight away, he started up again uninvited as only the over-educated and those devoid of any common sense can do.

'What is it exactly you want me to do Crowley?'

I thought it best not to tell him what I really wanted him to do in front of Derek and Joan, so I settled for second best and thus only the instructions for the race.

'Just do your civic duty tonight alongside your lovely missus and make sure the race starts with some pomp and circumstance bang on the dot at 9pm. You're the best we could do for a celebrity starter.'

With that, I spread the course map out on the large coffee table so all my visitors could see the road plan in detail.

'The race has never been run as late in the day as this before, so it is important everyone knows the route like the back of their hand.'

Nobody had questioned my motives for the twilight timings, believing only that I was trying to attract a larger crowd. Only Booby knew that the other essential character involved in my plan only worked nights!

'OK, listen up everybody. Starter's gun at 9pm from the slipway in front of the Sloop. Up through Fore Street and on past St EIA's Parish Church. Straight ahead, then across Lambeth Walk to Porthminster

Beach. Drop down onto the sand and then a pleasant swim to the harbour slipway, back to where we started.'

My fingers traced the route as I spoke. It wasn't complicated and pretty much the one raced every year. This time, however, the route passed by the church a little closer than normal thanks to the bright red and white race day tape that had been positioned to perfection following my detailed and insistent instructions.

'The RNLI will keep the night waters safe and bright,' said Derek.

Joan finished his assurances almost telepathically.

'Everywheres else will be lit up like Blackpool Illuminations and we're sure to expect the television and press people what with all the other stuff thas been going on around here latelys.'

Not to be outdone Lord Terrance gave the last word, finishing with an animated flourish.

'Plus we have a record number of competitors this year. It should be some night!'

I knew we could all count on this, if nothing else.

At 8.45pm Booby and I left the studio and ambled down the dimming back roads, carefully picking our way across the cobbles approaching the Sloop Inn from the Downalong end of town. I was smoking, not because I was nervous, although to be fair I should have been. Boobs was all a-flutter as he confirmed his recent activities.

'I did as you asked Ally. Chopper and his boys were only too happy to help after all the fun you provided them with the other night with those two poor policemen.'

As the Sloop came fully into view, a large, noisy crowd was gathered at the race starting point. There seemed to be as many participants in the men's competition that was primed to go first, as there were spectators, and the racers were strutting around in their garish wetsuits either warming up or showing off their lunchboxes. The sun was now low on the horizon, and it was a beautiful midsummer's evening. Pity we were working.

Lord and Lady Trivago, along with Derek and Joan Panalba, stood on a small wooden stage that had been erected to lend a little pomp and circumstance to the event and at their side sat the mayor who was in a wheelchair. I was pleased to see it looked like he had regained a little colour in his cheeks if not alas, his missing testicle. Lord Terrance raised a loudhailer to his mouth and with all the style of a man well accustomed to public speaking, began proceedings while his wife looked sideways on at him with a seething hatred in her eyes.

'On behalf of the organising committee, the mayor and of course my beautiful wife, I thank you all for such a great turnout.'

It was a good job it wasn't Tamsin holding the starting gun as although it was full of blanks, I am sure she would have at least pistol whipped him to death with it. The nation's media had, indeed, just as Joan predicted, turned out in force and the usual suspects Sky, The BBC, ITV, Radio 5 and even the normally lapsy daisy Radio Cornwall had appeared in pursuit of a headline. His Lordship continued, following a joyful burst of applause.

'Spectators from around the world make us all proud tonight by giving generously to our disaster fund and help us rebuild this lovely town and our reputation as the number one holiday destination of this proud land!'

With his rallying call complete, he raised the gun and without so much as a kiss my arse, he pulled the trigger and the startled competitors raced away down the quayside.

I'm not one for speeches so Booby and I hadn't hung around to hear his pontifications and just as the bang of the gun resonated around the town, we were arriving at the church to see IA standing ready and primed in the entryway. I, at least, knew what was coming. It was a bit like a good joke, always worth a second laugh and as I sniggered to myself, I also educated Booby, 'Let's stand by the memorial mate and enjoy the view.' The competitors came hurtling down Fore Street towards us, all still tightly packed as the spectators threw themselves into shop doorways and against the shopfronts to avoid being trampled. Film crews were at work from upper windows and other safer vantage points and with the streetlights blazing down like spotlights at the Super Bowl final, the whole scene looked like a cross between a night-time Formula One race and a Spanish bull run.

In the church doorway, out of sight of the masses, IA wind milled both her arms in opposite directions and the light around her glowed yellow once more and then, crash, bang, wallop, it was as if a firework had exploded early in its launch pad and out of the blinding flash and noise sprinted two stark bollock-naked and confused geezers whom I immediately recognised as the missing stroppy businessmen Phillip and Richard, now released from their concrete confinements. I am not sure how she did it, but the saint had somehow compelled them to run as if the devil himself was pursuing them and they took off like a couple of Walthamstow greyhounds on a promise, instantly leading the racecourse runners along the trail like seasoned pacemakers.

A much too good-looking blond surfer dude, who, up until that point was heading the contestants, pointed at the two disappearing pacey old farts and in reaction to the unplanned nudity made a simple observation followed by a call to arms that had hilarious consequences, 'Great idea guys! Get em off everybody!'

And with that, the majority of the runners stumbled about laughing and, still half running, stripped off. Some fell onto the cobbles, yet all were joining in the revelry while the stunned TV and radio correspondents looked on and made their reports. I heard the geezer from the BBC above all the others as he yelled into his microphone as if England had scored the winner in the World Cup final, 'The race has turned into a mass streak! Oh dear, oh dear, oh dear!'

Looking now at the rear of the racers as they made their chaotic way down from the Market Square, it was all bums and backs as they galloped onward toward

Porthminster Beach and the swim that awaited them there, three quarters of a mile away.

Once they were out of sight Booby and I made our way to the Guildhall and as we approached, the workman I had employed earlier in the proceedings stood in hard hat and overalls at the side of Barbara Hepworth's Dual Form sculpture. As soon as he recognised me he held out a large key.

'I did as you said Mr Crowley. The under stage is nice an' secure. Mind you I had to bung the caretaker a few quid.'

He was a mercenary bastard which was of course to my advantage, as I replied, 'Don't sweat it pal, I'll make it more than worth your while.'

As I breezed past into the hall I dropped a couple of hundred in tenners into his hand making the exchange for the key. He looked amazed rather than pleased, then to put him in his place Booby snubbed him, nose upturned, as he followed me inside. I shouted my final instructions back to the workman 'Don't spend it all at once son. Oh, and wait here if you want to double that.'

Once through the winding entrance way, we sauntered further into the hall and towards the stage at the far end.

We talked as we walked, 'Listen Boobs, my AIDS cure isn't exactly conventional medicine I'm afraid. You are going to have to have total faith in me tonight mate.'

His reply was sad, yet pragmatic, 'I haven't got anything to lose have I really Ally?'

I didn't mouth my reply, though I certainly thought it. Only your soul, my old mucker, only your soul. Booby began to get a little tearful, so once we had mounted the stage I thought it best to get straight down to the business end and take his mind off the impending jeopardy. I pointed at the taped crosses or 'spikes' on the stage used by previous actors as their positioning markers to ensure the correct choreography. Firstly, I pointed at a large red cross, 'I want you to stand here Boobs and no matter what happens, don't move, that is all I ask of you. Do you understand?'

He relocated bravely onto the mark, hardly noticing the large yellow cross six feet behind it, and stood to attention. Then he held his head up proudly and in a heartfelt murmur he declared, 'I, …I will not move. I, … I love you Ally.'

I walked away down the stage side steps choked, flicking my dog end into the auditorium and replied sincerely, 'I know you do mate, I know you do. Chins up, I'll be back in a mo.' I continued to the under-stage area, removing the chalk and candles from my coat pockets as I went because time was now tight, then I set about my workman-like business beneath where Booby stood like a statue. The bait was sorted up top, now all I needed to do was prime the trap with my chalked artistic renderings.

Booby had stood still for nearly three quarters of an hour by the time I had finished below the stage, so I knew I could trust him not to bottle it later. I slammed the door to the crypt-like area shut and turned the large key twice in the recently fitted oversized deadlock.

Booby's eyes were closed tight in meditation as I took my seat in the third row of the stalls, and as I lit a calming cigarette at 9.55pm our first guest of the evening, The Black Manilishi, entered stage right and joined Booby, contentedly curling himself around his ankles. 'Don't worry,' I addressed my disconcerted housemate, 'it's all cool, he's on our side.'

Looking at the entrance to the hall, I could tell it was pitch darkness outside and without ceremony the tall, thin figure of De Havilland appeared, walking gracefully in, to be rewarded with my discourteous welcome, 'Evening guvnor, I do like a punctual ghoul.'

His voice was suitably creepy as he churlishly retorted, 'Don't mock me Crowley, I will soon be strong enough to finish you if I wish.'

Waving my hand in invitation at the now transfixed and frightened donor whilst also pitching my legs over the chairs in front to demonstrate my confidence, I confirmed his words.

'Hopefully so. That's the deal old chum, I am guessing you're thirsty right?' And then in more of an insistent tone accompanied by a further specific indication toward my friend, I completed my statement, 'Have a drink on me!'

De Havilland never took his eyes off me, suspecting even at this late stage some sort of deception. Regardless no doubt, his need and greed took a hold of his senses and soon he was standing by Booby who was riveted to the spot in fear, his right foot upon the red cross. As the vampire scrutinised his prey, he disparagingly observed, 'Not a fine vintage I would imagine, but he will do, even if his disease sours my pleasure.'

'Beggars can't be choosers you ungrateful bastard,' I countered, 'anyway, bottoms up Drac, fill your boots!' It was hard to be jovial as the vampire seized Booby who had his eyes tightly shut and was holding his breath. De Havilland pushed my friend's head back to expose his chubby throat before diving in, fangs first. Booby slumped lifeless in the long, strong, sinewy arms that had him gripped vice-like, like a grateful lover. I was however, relieved to see that in time-honoured fashion, he had indeed fainted.

The Black Manilishi sat to the side, unflinching as the vampire enjoyed his first taste of human blood this century. The claret was dripping down all around Booby's chest expelled by his fast failing, previously high blood pressure. Thank goodness he was out like a light! De Havilland lowered Booby to the stage, still continuing to drain his life force, and I took the opportunity to join them onstage, the predator oblivious to my movements. Once Booby had been flat on his back for no more than a minute and I was sure that he was purged, I called last orders.

'Alright you greedy bastard eight pints is all you get!'

The vampire stood erect and bloodied, arms spread like he had just scored from a free kick and was waiting for the acclaim, so I pushed him gently backwards away from my prone friend and toward the yellow cross behind him on the stage floor.

'Ahhhhhhhhhhh Crowley!' He cried out refreshed, 'I feel the power returning to my veins.'

'Jolly good! Step back will you my old son, let the dog see the rabbit.' My request must have seemed reasonable because he took a couple more paces backward and now stood directly on the yellow cross. It was too late for him to react as I pointed the previously hidden remote control at his feet and pressed my thumb onto the small control pad button. 'Cheerio for now, fangs for the memories and all that, my son.' With my fond farewell ringing in his shell-like, the hidden stage trapdoor beneath him opened and he plummeted like a stone into the space below, accompanied with an unpleasant shocked look on his boat.

Looking down into the space through the narrowing gap, as the doors refitted to the stage, I could see the untidy landing had left him somewhat perplexed, I gave him a little information that I knew he would find interesting, 'I've decorated for you down there my old mate. Hope you like it, I'm sure it will at least keep you quiet for a while.' Once the doors had shut completely I heard him scream in terror, certain now that he had had a gander at all the signs and restraints I had chalked around his new lock-up as he knelt in sheer abjection.

Pressing a finger to Booby's blood-splattered neck I could still feel a very faint pulse and realised that I hadn't got long before it would disappear altogether. Throwing open the Guildhall's front doors, I yelled for the workman, who had indeed hung around awaiting another lucrative pay day. The sight of Booby unconscious, covered in blood and with The Black Manilishi opportunistically licking around the puncture wounds on his neck was almost enough to make you lose your lunch, but after shooing off the freebooter tomcat, my helper and I lifted the body, one at each end, and started our long stagger down the cobbled back streets towards St EIA's Parish Church.

I was sweating like a rapist when we arrived at the entrance way. The streets were abandoned as all and sundry had followed the race event and the evening was now cloaked in darkness, except of course the open church interior which the Black Manilishi dashed into ahead of us, as if happy to be home. The mass streak had, as intended, been the perfect diversion spell. Inside her house of worship IA stood adorned in full battle dress before the large stained window that venerated her glory. I noticed immediately that two of the fonts' angel cavities were now vacant. It seemed that so far things were going exactly to plan. The saint spoke without ceremony.

'Bring him to me.'

We staggered those last few yards and lay our gentle, but grossly overweight, fallen comrade down as elegantly as we could at her feet.

'My pleasure,' was the best I could muster, calves and forearms burning with the strain.

The workman looked worn to a frazzle so I placed another couple of hundred in his hand and told him softly, 'Here you go mate. Mum's the word, eh?'

'Don't yuh, yuh… yuh worry mister. I ain't seen a thing!' was his stuttering reply and then he was off like a bat out of hell.

IA knelt alongside my horizontal friend while the Black Manilishi sat respectfully by his head. Booby's breathing was no longer perceptible and gravely concerned, I could only implore the saint, 'Better work your voodoo Mrs, he's nearly gone!'

Her sword now rotated in her grip to resemble the form of a cross, and now it was balancing on its point unsupported. She reached out to touch both Booby and the cat.

'Turn your head magician,' she commanded looking up from her now kneeling position. I didn't argue and as soon as I had obeyed her command there was a blinding flash of light that engulfed the space around me accompanied by the sound and fury of a mini hurricane. Flash, bang, wallop, what a picture! Soul transfusion accomplished!

Turning slowly once the ambience had settled, I saw a traumatised Booby pulling himself up by his elbows and the cat lying dead beside him, its tongue exposed and eyes wide open but inert. IA, as expected, was nowhere to be seen. Supporting the shell-shocked and silent Booby away and back out onto the road, it seemed more than just a pity that the cat had died even if it was in the line of duty and to save my friend's life.

With De Havilland under the Guildhall stage, I knew that I was on borrowed time. I had arranged to keep his three slinky wives out of the picture thanks to Chopper and his pals who, earlier that night, had thrown an old fishing net around the abandoned building up on the headland to create a temporary zoo. The best I could hope for was that it would take the vampire at least till dawn to free himself and then he would be just in time to fry in the daylight, but I knew that that would be most unlikely. Sooner rather than later I was sure he would come looking for his revenge.

By the time we reached the Sloop, the benches outside were crammed full of race spectators, all highly animated and awfully pissed, as the first contestant to finish, exited the waves in a glare of spotlights, completely naked and with half a dozen other like-minded nudists close behind. He burst through the finishing tape and everyone cheered and clapped as he carried straight on into the pub for a pint.

'How are you feeling mate?' I inquired of the now independent Booby who seemed to have perked up no end. 'Let's have a drink hey? I bet you could do with a pick me up after what you have been through tonight, hey?' Entering the door, he slapped me hard on the back and delivered his answer, one which came as a massive surprise and also in a much gruffer, deeper voice than normal, 'Pick me up! Bloody right! Let's see if we can pick up some totty!'

It was a full voltage shock. Something fundamental had changed regarding my housemate's disposition. It seemed it wasn't just the well-being of the cat trapped, now released Mr William Nancarrow which was now implanted within him due to the transfusion, but that Booby had also taken on all the less savoury characteristics of the wayward young man from two hundred years before.

He gave an enormous, 'Ooooooooarrrrrrrrrrh!' As he approached the bar and I in return gave a very quiet, 'oh fuck!'

Part Six

Burn Baby Burn

The studio apartment looked like it had taken a direct hit during the Blitz!

I sat slumped with my head in my hands on one of the still remaining upstanding kitchen chairs, elbows on the table, which was a mass of empty bottles, cigarette packets, glasses and foodstuffs in all possible variants of consumption. The ashtray in front of my banging head resembled a shrine of burnt offerings as I added my last tombstone on earth to the pyre. It was 11.30am three days after the midsummer night jamboree and the apartment had been party central non-stop since. Booby was lying face down in his boxers and vest with one leg hanging over the side of the bed like a drunken speedway rider, while I sat watching him snoring à la worn-out warthog.

It seemed a distant memory, him dancing, balanced precariously on a dining table, a bottle in each hand at the Queen's Hotel. The whole clientele were paralytic, celebrating the fun and success of the Biathlon and boogieing on down at his side was the women's race winner complete with her victory sash, which proclaimed her position in big red letters as 'First!' Other than that, all she had had on were her skimpy red bikini bottoms. They say a Leopard can't change its spots, but I would have had to disagree. The once gentle, over-effeminate Mr Booby de Faux had turned into Oliver Reed on steroids as the spirit of the Black Manilishi raged and raved on through his bloodstream into the night. I was further reminded of his new lease of life and the one hundred and eighty degree change in his sexual preferences, as while trying to enjoy a quiet cigarette around the back of the hotel, I caught sight of him banging the arse off the newly crowned Biathlon champion using the wheelie bin behind her as a bump stop! It was all very bizarre as he didn't look any different outwardly, but judging from his performance, it seemed not only had his tastes changed, but that he also knew how to use his equipment as would have been expected of a true eighteenth-century cocksman.

Standing over his now prone body, by the look on his sleeping face, he was probably reliving the memories in his depraved dreams. Whatever was inside him needed to grow up fast or at least slow down or I feared IA would soon be looking for another cat!

Leaving him to his beauty sleep, I had decided a walk would probably clear my head, hence I headed out onto the familiar uneven cobbles of the back road and onward to Trivago's Guest House, imagining that Lady Muck was probably resting, glad to be away from the last couple of days' revelries herself.

Rapping quietly on the door, trying to avoid a brain haemorrhage, it wasn't long before Tamsin popped her head out through the access, though she kept the gap suspiciously narrow. At first I thought she was almost certainly half-dressed and trying to maintain her dignity as she spoke, clearly surprised by my appearance, 'Oh! Hello Alex.'

It wasn't the reception I was expecting. 'Cuppa tea would be nice darlin.'

Her face reddened as the door remained ajar. I noticed her recently replaced wedding ring and heard an unexpected voice behind her. 'Is that my driver dear? I told him midday. Tell the scoundrel to wait in the car will you, I will be out soon enough.'

Lord Terrance fucking Trivago was back in the house! Seemed like he had reclaimed his significant other. I could only walk away in anger as Lady Tamsin shouted after me, exposing a little more of her naked body in the doorway than was sensible, 'I'm sorry Alex! I am sure you understand. He is still my husband!'

I understood alright, after all. It was a class thing when it came down to the nitty gritty, blokes likes me were only good for a bit of friction it appeared.

Ever pragmatic, I thought it best to get some cigarettes and approaching the Norse Stores, I observed the buxom Mandy Contattio fitting some flowers into the wire display rack outside the shop. She hadn't seen me coming, that is until a large bodybuilding type of geezer, exited the shop doorway and raised the alarm.

'What the fuck you want boy? Ain't you done enough damage round 'ere?'

The question was not wasted on me and of course more than fair, but I couldn't pretend to appreciate his menacing tone. Considering I only just about came up to his chin, he seemed surprised when I issued my advice.

'Step aside pinhead before you get hurt, I only want some fags.'

He didn't, it seemed, want to debate the issue and without further ado, he swung a right hook my way, but as is normally the case with the large, musclebound and stupid, he was too slow. Moving swiftly inside his punch I brought my right knee up hard into his groin. I'm not sure where his balls went, but his eyeballs nearly popped out of his head at the surprise impact.

Gravity did its job as always and he was instantly rolling around on the road in agony as I stepped over his writhing body and forwards into the shop, alas overconfidently forgetting about the curvy minx who was still primed and ready to go outside.

'Do us a six pack Mands, will you please? I'm gasping.'

I had uttered my request without looking behind me, not realising she was closing in fast welding an umbrella taken from the nearby courtesy rack.

'You bastard! I'll knock your fuckin' brains out!' was her best counter offer, instead of a much needed but not really expected, 'Hi Ally, good to see you,' and she brought the parasol down with some unladylike force about my head. Luckily, she only delivered a glancing blow, though her momentum took her straight past me as I dodged her off balance bod and she crashed headlong into the shop counter, scattering all and sundry about the gaff. Lying on her back on the floor, I was amused to see she had got red knickers on but I was less enthused to see the likewise red droplets of blood dripping to my feet from the head wound she had inflicted. Even in those circumstances, I am pleased to say I was ever the gentleman as I enlightened the fallen gangster's daughter, 'I'll give you that one darlin.

I probably deserved it, but don't push any further, huh?'

Lucky I guess to be walking away from the mêlée with at least some pride intact as well as the oversized packet of cigarettes, while Mandy helped her new knucklehead boyfriend to his knees.

The flow of claret stemmed soon enough, although I could feel the pressure of the swelling beneath my palm predicting another headache to replace the one that had only just subsided. My only real regret though was that I hadn't obtained a carrier bag, as the nuisance ciggy six-pack was a bloody awkward lump to carry without one.

Not wanting to return to the studio apartment just yet, a protracted walk was still in order. The Sloop's punters seemed happy enough, sitting outside enjoying the sunshine along with their liquid refreshments, and a few of the punters raised their glasses and jeered in a friendly way as I passed by, bloodied but unbowed. Seemingly, and I must admit pleasingly, my reputation was on the up. I decided on an unlikely trot to the church, thinking I might make midweek, midday mass, as always, one of my favourite heresies. The now re-opened Glory Hole, with its new colourful sign in the window, invited all and sundry to 'Come inside and browse at leisure'. Phillip Browne stood outside chatting happily to a few potential customers, quite the bon ami. Saluting him as I passed by with, 'Morning guv!' he replied, 'Hiya Alex, good to see you old pal!' Another leopard indeed, but this time this one pleasantly had changed its spots the right way around.

It wasn't long before I approached the studio shop of Richard Soul, where he stood outside, taking a family picture portrait with his ancient but top quality Nikon camera. Mum, Dad and two nippers stood in prearranged domestic postures. They all had huge smiles on their faces and Richard was clearly happy in his work. He gave me a pleasant wave as I meandered by. I don't know what their holy incarceration had done to them exactly, but I couldn't help think how good it would be for the British Prison Service, if they could 'Bottle it' and do the same, converting previous miscreant arseholes into such pleasant citizens as Phillip and Richard now seemed to be.

The lump on my head was soon at its zenith and away from any onlookers, I entered the parish church. So far this day I had been beaten up, blown out and pleasantly surprised so I figured the score was 2-2, could I go on and bag the winner I wondered? Moving to the front of the aisle, I looked up at the magnificent stained-glass window and the image of IA and although there were a few solitary folk silently praying or in contemplation amongst the pews, nobody gave me a second glance as I took my seat on the end bench of the first row. Parallel across the aisle sat the saint herself, in her now familiar modern guise plus backpack.

'You have been fighting magician?'

'Just a slight misunderstanding that's all, no harm done really.'

With that we turned to look each other directly in the eye as she probed further with the question I was dreading.

'How is your house guest Mr de Faux?'

Even so I was relieved she brought the subject up as I replied, 'He's err, not what I expected!'

'No, I suppose not. The spirit of The Black Manilishi does not fit so naturally well within your friend then I assume?'

'Too bloody well! He's a little bit wild to say the least. Any chance we could have the old Booby back?'

From the front bench, she moved gracefully into the Lady Chapel and stood touching Barbara Hepworth's Madonna and Child sculpture. This icon represented a requiem for those that had been lost before their natural time and as I stood watching her from behind, she uttered the words I was hoping to hear, 'Well, we cannot have such unruliness in one as gentle as Mr de Faux can we? We would be back to square one and the Manilishi's sacrifice would have been in vain would it not? Godspeed, Mr Crowley.'

I knew when I wasn't wanted so without further ado, I departed the church and made my way to the quayside café that had quickly become my home from home. Through the open patio doors I watched as the holidaymakers packed the harbour walkways. The beaches were still cordoned off by the barbed wire barricades. Recent events had at least been Box Office enough to draw the day-trippers.

Normally a pretty woman would not have gone unnoticed, only as Maggie brought my second cappuccino over, I wondered how, up until this point, I had not detected her obvious charms, but now, as I thanked her, they had entered my radar in a big way.

'Thanks Mags, any chance of one of your beautiful sausage rolls? I love the pastry, how do you do it?'

She recognised a charmer when she saw one and her bullshit detector kicked in.

'You're very polite today Alex. Feeling guilty or something?'

The smile on her face as she walked away made it obvious to those seated around that she had at least put me in my place. She was right, of course, only I wasn't about to go soft as I watched her wiggle away. She looked amazed as she retrieved the fifty pound tip I had left in the saucer. Normally I would have thrust it down a waitress's cleavage, but she was much too nice to appreciate that sort of behaviour.

'Keep the change darlin', oh and thanks for the guidance. See you soon, I hope?' her smile made it clear that she got my drift.

As I walked away, lighting yet another cigarette, I wondered if the sleeping de Faux beauty was up and about, then as I entered the studio five minutes later, not only was he up, but fussing around in his pinny sporting a huge feather duster. I was further flabbergasted to see the transformation from party central back to the immaculate Boho chic of the previous week. Booby stopped momentarily upon my entry, then pointed out in his erstwhile effeminate voice and also in no uncertain terms, 'Oh Ally! Come in quickly don't let the dust in love, it's taken me hours to clean up after all the mess you seem to have made these last few days.' It was more than a relief to see him back to his old self, but also now in vigorous health thank goodness, well thanks to IA.

The rest of the week passed in domestic bliss and having never been married, I suspected this was what it was supposed to be like, according to the guidebooks at least. Our arrangement was however a little unconventional though it seemed to work like a charm. Tonight was date night. Dating was not my usual method of getting to know a woman. In the past I had picked up skirt wherever and whenever, so as I splashed the aftershave on, I felt doubly pleased with myself that I had gone about this occasion in a more formal and conventionally acceptable way, having actually asked the divine Maggie out for a meal.

At 7.30pm on the dot, I arrived outside the café and there waiting hand on hip and with a hesitant expression, she stood in black jeggings, boots and T-shirt. I was the first to break the ice, 'I wasn't sure you would show darlin'.'

'No, me neither. I am really not sure this is a good idea.'

Her reply was at least honest, if not exactly inspiring.

It was however more than enough encouragement for me, so with a courteous wave of my arm I motioned toward the walkway in the direction of the town's entertainments, 'After you ma'am, the night is young, and our table awaits.'

Putting her arm through mine, she attached a caveat.

'Don't make me regret this Alex. Please.'

We chatted easily and naturally enough as we made our way across the harbour and onwards toward the far Porthminster Beach and the foreshore restaurant that I had pre-booked, hoping my romantic efforts would enamour me sufficiently to allay any doubts in her mind. Of course that was an unrealistic ambition considering the chaos the area and its populace had suffered since my arrival.

We were soon seated inside at a romantic window table. Our waiter, who was Italian looking and wary of me, rather than attentive, arrived to take our order, 'What can I get you folks to drink?'

I had noticed the cocktail menu and as it would have been a shame not to, ordered without any further polite consultation.

'Two Dry Martinis please, shaken not stirred.'

The date was a great success, the food was superb, the wine splendid and the bill suitably eye watering. It was delightful to be surrounded by people who were similarly happy, that not being my normal Saturday night audience, and it really was a shame to leave.

Again, we walked arm in arm back across the town and had a few more drinks in a number of the friendly and weekender-packed pubs of St Ives, but as the midnight bells of St EIA's rang out, we were standing now awkwardly outside Maggie T's Café, neither of us knowing what would happen next. 'This is me,' she confirmed.

'What does the T stand for? I take it it's not just a play on words,' I said not wanting the evening to end.

'Nothing that clever Alex, just my married name I'm afraid. Taylor,' she playfully responded.

'Herm, interesting,' my equally playful response, so not wanting to push my luck too far I planted a kiss on her lips, "See you soon?"

She didn't need to think too hard thankfully and girlishly replied, 'I hope so.' With that, I was away feeling strangely elated for such a seasoned womaniser. Maybe in this town she would be my third time lucky, I thought conceitedly.

Contentment is not an emotion I'm much used to, so as I sat on the bench in Norway Square enjoying my final cigarette of the night before turning in, the last thing I was expecting, lost deep in my thoughts, was pious company. IA had entered the Square unobserved and was now seated next to me as my senses returned to the here and now.

'Had a nice time Mr Crowley?'

'Yes, thank you ma'am, very nice indeed.'

She continued with the thread, 'It is pleasant is it not, to live with some sort of semblance of normality?'

I couldn't deny that, 'Yes, it is. I don't normally get the chance.'

She had made me comprehend my own point, so satisfied with her efforts, took her leave. 'Then take your chance magician, although beware!'

The saint disappeared from view before I had taken her words in fully and as I looked toward the harbour, my inner defences rose as I contemplated her final words. I could, of course, get used to this genteel and superior lifestyle, but as always, there had to be something sinister coming around the corner. At that time, I couldn't possibly have imagined what this could be, although all the clues were there nevertheless.

My imagination didn't need to fill in many of the gaps, as later I was told reliably what had happened behind my back as I left my evening's date at her quayside home-cum-business. Maggie had entered her living quarters at the rear of the café and thrown her keys happily upon the sofa. Regrettably, that is where the pleasurable part of her evening ended. A man was seated upon her occasional chair. Although she was surprised, it wasn't alarm in her voice as she questioned him.

'Hello Terrance, I see you still have your key then?'

'It is my property still Sis, so why wouldn't I?'

Resigned to her late-night brotherly visit, Maggie put the kettle on but did not inquire if her sibling wanted a cup of tea as she had noticed he was sitting aside a bottle of whiskey with a half-full glass in hand. She was also sure it wasn't his first of the evening, as he had waited patiently for her return.

He looked over-comfortable as she addressed him again, 'I'll pay you back Terrance, I just need a bit more time that's all,' she pleaded.

Ungraciously he laughed before he commented, 'I doubt it dearest. This place must be worth a cool mil by now. That's a lot of cheesecake and coffee I'm afraid.'

Standing, her back to him and supporting her trembling frame on the sink sides, she began to cry as the truth and hopelessness of his words sank in.

'Don't cry Sis. Do this little thing for me and all your financial woes will be over once and for all. You don't owe Crowley anything and as long as you use your married name he won't tie you in with me until it is far too late.'

'I don't like it Terrance,' she appealed, 'He seems like such a decent guy.'

His Lordship nearly choked with rage as he countered, 'A decent guy! He was responsible for Bucca's death! Lillo is going to be banged up for years! Two of our best loved local businessmen disappear for weeks and then come back unrecognisable, all wishy-washy and socially aware!'

Rising to his feet angered, his words turned into a hateful rant, 'Then, we have a bloody shark attack at our biggest event of the year, followed by various other animal assaults all over the shop, at one of which, our honourable mayor has one of his balls lopped off!' It was all he could do to catch his breath as he turned apoplectic, 'Next we have a fucking tidal wave!' The self-important lord made for the door, but continued, his voice getting ever higher as his wrath boiled over, 'My business associate from London is then crushed under our famous ancient monument which is unceremoniously demolished by my very own Bentley! Two of our finest policemen are also hospitalised following a vicious attack by his biker friends and then last week we have two hundred beatniks streaking bollock naked through the town at our previously esteemed and prestigious Biathlon. The shame of it all!' Turning in the doorway and pointing at his sister and with some venom he made his final climatic point, 'And then to cap it all, he shagged the arse off my wife! A decent guy! I'll be in touch, keep your hand on your ha'penny if you know what's good for you my dear!'

And with that he left, slamming the door behind him.

Sunday morning and the studio apartment was flooded with bright sunlight as Booby and I enjoyed our breakfast in peace. 'Cor, it's hot today Ally,' said my already perspiring friend and housemate.

Looking out at the beach and the barricades, I lamented, 'Pity we can't go for a swim mate.'

'Probably get arrested if we tried.'

Tidying the breakfast things away, pottering about in our domestic bliss, my phone began to ring and I was soon smiling into the receiver as I replied, 'Hi Mags. Tonight? Yeah, that sounds cool. Meet you at eight then. The Crypt Gallery it is. Ciao baby!'

Booby had earwigged the conversation, 'She seems like a nice girl. Going anywhere nice?'

I was somewhat lost in the St Ives Times and Echo as he asked his question, reading all about the Biathlon streak, with the front-page featuring Lord and Lady

Trivago looking crestfallen and side-lined by the large attention-grabbing caption, 'I've never been so ashamed'. Smiling inwardly, I remembered the query that had been left hanging in the air and answered him, 'Errr, some sort of charity art auction at the Crypt Gallery I think.'

Just like a proud mum, he responded, 'Oh that sounds super-duper dear.'

As the evening sun went down on that glorious day, I stood suited and booted in the gallery entrance, rightly warned by Booby that these events tended to be a little formal. Chopper and a dozen of his mates thundered past on their bikes and cheered embarrassingly my way when they spotted me in my Sunday best. I was, however, assured they were good to their mothers.

An anxious looking Maggie in her little black dress, heels and the obligatory pearl necklace approached waving her hands nervously in my direction, so gently pulling on her wrists when she was within striking distance, I pecked her on both cheeks and then placed my hands on her shoulders to dish out my compliments, 'You look beautiful Mags, quite the belle of the ball.'

Her smile seemed forced and a small tremor in her voice was evident as she self-consciously replied, 'Th… thanks, I do my best.'

Her best was more than good enough for me, but something was wrong, therefore I began to investigate gently, 'You alright luv? You look a little shaky.'

She avoided my eyes as she responded. 'Yes, yes, just a bit of a headache, that's all. Sorry.' She didn't need to apologise and that made me even more suspicious as we made our way up the outside stairs to the gallery entrance. 'Come on Alex they'll be waiting.'

That seemed a peculiar thing for her to say so I delved again, 'Who's they?' Which she brushed off clumsily with, 'Oh no one really, I just meant the other guests.' I doubted I was being oversensitive, but I gave her the benefit of the doubt and followed her into the spacious gallery. I must admit that as I chucked my cigarette butt into the gutter outside, I also instinctively checked the building for alternative entrances and exits, as only those who have experienced dramatic interludes tend to do as a matter of course and good sense.

A tall, skinny man, smartly dressed and with grey wavy hair, stood at the entrance as if he were greeting guests at a wedding reception. Extending his arms he proclaimed, 'Welcome to the Crypt Gallery my friends.

You are just in time for the auction. Please take a seat, there are a few left right at the front.'

I sensed the gathering's eyes burning into my back as we made our way to the front row. It was a better than good turnout and it was also obvious the majority of the people there knew who I was and what I had been up to recently, for they muttered and murmured amongst themselves as, warily, I took my place. At the very front of the room behind a battered old rostrum stood a wild-haired, half-shaven comedic presence with round wire rimmed glasses holding an antique gavel like a conductor holds his baton.

'Good evening everyone, my name is Stevey Stevens and I am one of the local directors of the Tate St Ives and proud to be your host and auctioneer tonight.'

A polite round of applause followed, but it didn't last long as he continued in the friendly way that instantly endeared him to his audience.

'Welcome, welcome, welcome. Tonight we are raising funds for a great and much needed cause and that is to repair the roof on this old chapel and keep our members and their paintings dry for everybody to enjoy long into the future.'

He indicated all the canvases and paraphernalia piled up around him.

'This is a fantastic opportunity for all of you here tonight to own a piece of original art from the very heart of this famous and historic society. Please, open your minds to abstraction and more importantly open your wallets, I beseech you. Firstly though, let me introduce you to my assistant tonight, she is a lovely lady and I do mean 'Lady'. Please welcome Lady Tamsin Trivago who has been kind enough to support our cause from the off and whose presence here tonight is both an honour and much appreciated.'

The applause was a little more forthcoming than earlier. Again, it wasn't like Led Zeppelin had taken to the stage as her ladyship, dressed to kill in short kilt, pop open white blouse and her hair up higher than her heels joined our excited host beside the rostrum. Throwing me a look that could have frozen a waterfall, Lady T addressed her flock, 'Thank you Mr Stevens. It is a great pleasure for me to be with you here tonight. Bless you all for helping to repair this charming place. Please Mr Stevens do proceed.'

Tamsin bent over to hoist high the first painting and what nearly fell out of her blouse looked a whole lot more interesting than the large picture she struggled to raise and then place on the viewing easel at her side. The picture looked to me like someone had thrown up on the canvas, spread it around with their foot, shoved it in a fancy frame and let it fester. As I rolled my eyes to the back of my head, I caught a glimpse of the small white clock on the wall. It was only 8.15pm.

Stevey Stevens quickly piped back in, 'This first piece is by one of our visiting artists this summer, Mr Spider Crab and it's called 'Goblin'. I am sure you will agree it is most impressive. Can we start the bidding at two thousand pounds, please?'

My abiding thought at the time was, 'Fuck, this is going to be a long night!'

Two hours later, Maggie and I exited the gallery along with all the other excited new owners of reputed artistic excellence. She squeezed my free arm as under the other one I had a large frame and canvas covered with brown wrapping paper.

'Oh Alex you shouldn't have! It's wonderful and I just love it,' she enthused.

I was a little surprised myself to be honest as I hadn't got her down as a culture vulture.

'Yeah triffic,' I countered, feigning similar appreciation. 'Come on, we can still get a few rounds in if we hurry.'

Five minutes later we sat together in the Union pub which was jam-packed, listening to a long blonde haired geezer strangling a tune out of his guitar. The painting lay against my legs as I enjoyed my pint and Maggie sipped her wine, still psyched about her oil and canvas present while the singer song killer worked his way through his repartee. Ironically, I picked the lyrics out somewhat poignantly as he sang, 'Art for art's sake. Money for God's sake.'

Maggie's voice returned me from my contemplations, 'That was exciting Alex, I thought the bidding was never going to stop on my piece.'

'Hey, it's only money,' I responded in mock horror, making my way to the bar desperate for another couple of drinks to anaesthetise my financial and audio pains.

The singer had finished his song and as he re-tuned his guitar, he engaged with the good-natured crowd, 'That last one was by 10cc and reached number five in 1975. Anybody got any requests for our last few songs?'

It was an offer I couldn't refuse, 'Hey! How about God Save the Queen mate, the Sex Pistols version. That got to number one in 1977!'

I didn't think he would have the bottle, but times they are a changing and he looked over to where I had now re-seated and officiously corrected me in front of all and sundry. 'Number two actually chummy! Anyway, I will certainly have a go for you.' He looked ultra-pleased with himself as he hit the first few chords and then most of the crowd looked horrified as he belted out the opening lyrics, 'God save the Queen, the fascist regime, that made you a moron......' I sank my pint truly contented as the Cornish songster smiled over at me. They don't write them like that anymore!

We fell out of the front door of the pub well past midnight much the worse for wear, along with the rest of the holidaymakers who had enjoyed the entertainment and who now made their noisy way back to their classy holiday lets. This evening had left me uncustomarily off guard, but even so, I was more than aware at the time that we were being watched by the two unhealthy looking scrotes, Flotsam and Jetsam. It was, apparently, their mission that night to observe and report back and soon they were sitting in the Hotel Trivago lounge doing just that, plus enjoying a couple of buckshee pints supplied by their new employer, Lord Terrance Trivago who sat opposite them, cross-legged and with his hands in the steeple position, anxious for their news. Once they had settled, he began, 'Gentlemen, please give me your bulletin.'

Flotsam took the lead in his West Country drawl. 'Well Crowley he do look handsome loved up with your sister m'lud,' and then Jetsam continued in support, 'Yeah they was all lovey dovey like.'

Still posed in his contemptuous grace, the noble tested the pair further. 'Excellent. I take it he didn't see either of you spying on him then?'

Jetsam seemed insulted, 'No Sir, I can assure you he only 'ad eyes for her.'

Lord Terrance stood up, putting his hands behind him like a visiting royal and now looking away into the darkness of the harbour, probed again. 'And the picture, did he have the picture?'

'Oh yes m'lud he had it under 'is arm and he paid a pretty price for it an' all,' Flotsam confirmed smugly.

'Jolly good, chaps. I won't detain you any longer, I will however require you to keep close quarters with our unsuspecting conjuror for the rest of the night, but don't let him see you skulking in the shadows will you?' The lord's instructions were simple and dismissive.

The two scruffs were soon back out on the back roads again, but no sooner had they exited the front door, another more dignified creature entered the back one and this time Lord Terrance was addressing a man much more in line with his social standing and one who had clearly overheard the conversation he had just concluded.

'You heard all that I assume? It seems he bought your painting as planned,' confirmed the snide aristocrat to the vampiric fiend who had just arrived.

'Oh yes, Sir Terrance, my kind has excellent hearing, I can assure you,' said the smiling De Havilland. He was dressed smartly in a black three piece suit and his long hair made him look like a taller, broodier Jim Morrison doppelganger. He was I admit, a handsome beast, but a beast all the same and one who was plotting alongside his patron on holding a revengeful reunion with yours truly.

'Thank you for your help Lord Terrance. You must truly hate Crowley with some passion?'

'It is more of an urge my dear boy, an urge to wipe him from the face of this planet!'

The vampire smiled sweetly, 'I will see to it personally, after all I owe you a debt of gratitude,' and with that he turned and concluded their brief chat as he left the room, 'I thank you again Lord Terrance, you are a man of much commendation. Until we meet again at sundown tomorrow, my friend.'

There was much I didn't know at that time and De Havilland's Guildhall liberation was far simpler than I could have imagined. My workman friend who had constructed the vampire's temporary cell under the

Guildhall stage on my behalf had also been busy selling his arse elsewhere on that evening. It seems I wasn't the only one he had drawn wages from that night. I should of course have known there was always more than one key to any lock and this second key had been purchased in educated speculation by His Lordship. From that evening till this, unseen by me, his two scruffy servants had been watching my every move for days and reporting them back, just as they would later fill me in on events thus far. Lord Terrance knew I was up to something and reasoned that if I wanted something secure it would be a good investment on his behalf to have access to it.

I don't suppose for a minute that Lord Terrance, as he watched my mercenary builder acquaintance and I struggle away with Booby's overweight, near lifeless body, on our way down the road to our rendezvous with IA at the church, that when he opened the door beneath the stage he would be confronted with a terrified and crouching child of the undead. My trap could only ever have been temporary and this new, unexpected meeting was mutually beneficial. Lord Terrance was no fool and also versed with at least an amateur's knowledge of the occult. He had pulled De Havilland bodily away from the signs and symbols that held him petrified, out into the darkness outside the hall, where the vampire had slowly recovered his wits.

At the same time as I was celebrating Booby's re-animation and good health in the Sloop, Lord Terrance and De Havilland had returned to the hotel where the lord kept his personal suite and established their friendship, immediately dedicating it to my destruction. The vampire was keen to reacquaint himself with me one conclusive and final time before he returned to the more luxuriant feeding grounds of the capital city, but he knew that he would need an unhindered approach or personal invite to gain entry into the studio apartment that I had transformed into a safe haven, thinking rightly that the majority of my nights would be spent indoors for the foreseeable, when not safely surrounded by others.

De Havilland understood the power and effectiveness of a 'Supernatural Portal' so they hatched a plan to place such a gateway inside my seaside dwelling. A clandestine doorway, he could leap out of at the appropriate time and then having negated the invitation clause a vampire needed for entry, bludgeon me to death in my own gaff. It was of course genius and all I had to go on at the time was the feeling that something wasn't quite right with Maggie. I normally trust my guts. That uneasy feeling has saved my life on many previous occasions, so as I sat up in bed with Maggie lying asleep next to me, it was past 3am and I recognised the old spider senses were tingling again. I had spent the last few hours in the flat above the café as our goodnight kiss had turned into an early hours bonk. The nail in the wall that hung the new painting wasn't the only thing I had banged in that night, but the picture on the wall was as crooked as it was ugly, hanging there on the piss. Beholding it in the dim moonlight streaming in through the open blinds, I couldn't fathom why it had been titled 'Goblin'. The name Spider Crab seemed familiar and maybe somehow associated with the title. I knew there was bound to be a reason and then I saw the signature in the right lower corner. Two initials, DH. I knew it wasn't David Hockney at least. Spider Crab and Goblin? Two associated nicknames from a wartime bomber? Then it struck me, a De Havilland Vampire Bomber!

My bed mate had woken. Smiling at me, she pulled herself in close, noticing I was eyeing the painting. 'It has got something ephemeral about it Alex,' she said dreamily.

'You mean it looks like it's been dashed out in ten minutes more like?'

Pulling the sheet self-consciously neck high, she sat upright aside me and then playfully whispered, 'I'm sure it was a labour of love.'

Labour of love or not, it was time for me to go, so I made my excuses.

'Gotta fly Mags. I don't want to leave Booby on his own too much at the moment. He's a little, errr, tender.'

By the time I had one foot in a trouser leg, she was at my side naked and holding me tight.

'It was a lovely night, Alex. It has been, a long time since, well you know!'

'Bloody hell girl! I wouldn't want to catch you practising then,' I hoped my words would boost her self-confidence if nothing else, as she shyly giggled and then asked me uneasily, 'I wondered if you could do me a favour Alex? Take the painting with you please. I am in the middle of decorating this room and I want an excuse to see you again anyway.'

I was a little bewildered, but also peculiarly intrigued by the painting. I also firmly believed it best to keep your possible enemies close so I complied with her strange wish, although at that time I hadn't grasped the big picture.

'Sure, but you don't need an excuse luv.'

The night had been most enjoyable, and I walked away with the clicking of the café door in the background and the painting wrapped in a brown paper covering under my arm. It seemed that maybe as far as women were concerned, in this town, it may well have been third time lucky after all.

By the time I crept silently into the studio I had concluded unkindly that the best place for the framed monstrosity was probably in the lav, but on second thought, I didn't want it to put me off what was often the most enjoyable task of my day. Passing Booby's open bedroom door, I could hear him playing the nose trumpet. I placed the painting on the floor, leaning it against the wall that lay dead adjacent to, but some distance from the entrance of my own room and unwrapped it. Sitting Buddha-like in front of it, I gazed fully into the abstract image and suddenly everything clicked.

Lifting it up slowly and deliberately, I positioned it on the wall as if trying to pick out the best place to hang it. There was an obvious spot so for a couple of minutes I held it stationary purposely giving it a chance to view its new surroundings, before putting it back on the floor. It was left leaning, looking across to my room. For a while I sat on the end of my bed smoking, staring at the canvas. I was giving the picture, which I now fully understood to be a portal of some sort, the opportunity to review its new surroundings. Taking the final drag on my cigarette, I flicked the light switch off and shut the bedroom door. I never did like a nosy bastard!

Outside the studio apartment all this time Flotsam and Jetsam, who mistakenly believed that I had not noticed them, were talking. Jetsam went first.

'Well, Lord Terrance was right, he took the painting in wif him alrighty.'

'Yes,' replied Flotsam, 'Looks like e's in for the night now. We might as well go gets some shut eye mate. We'll tell 'is Lordship we stayed all night, hah, hah, hah!'

They were soon gone, mistaken in their assumptions as I still sat bolt upright on the end of my bed. I didn't know De Havilland had an artistic streak, but I certainly knew he had a sadistic one. I knew also by that time the vampire was probably inspecting the boring domestic view through his side of the portal. He would be studying the studio sitting room through to the opposite side of the barred bedroom door, taking in every detail and planning his forthcoming surprise entrance and attack. He would, I am sure have innocently thought I had closed the door to drown out the din of Booby's nasal melodies.

It was now 3.30am and as dawn was closer than any self-respecting cold-blooded parasite would consider timely, I knew I was safe, for now at least. He was probably going to attack me tomorrow night right here in the studio, now that I had misguidedly invited him in by innocently conveying the painting inside as a welcome proxy guest. It seemed my evening date had all been a Machiavellian set-up and at this point it was now totally clear why, nonetheless, I decided to stick the pondering about Maggie's part in the deception on the backburner as I leapt out onto the beach from the rear of the property's balcony. The tide was right in, and the cold sea lapped around my ankles, still, I reasoned it was better to be a little bit wet than a whole lot dead.

Ten minutes later, having left the beach to the front of the Tate, I was now on Back Road knocking on the front door of a tiny fisherman's cottage that was also the haunt of the first piece in my jigsaw, the facetious auctioneer who had sold me a pup in the first place, Stevey bloody Stevens. The auctioneer opened his door dressed in a silk dressing gown and bunny rabbit slippers and squinted at me in the darkness issuing his inquiry, 'Who! What! Is going on?'

Putting my hand on his face like a rugby player executing a handoff, I pushed him with some force back into his property. 'You tell me mate,' I demanded, as I was infuriated, though even then I suspected this buffoon had not purposely put me in danger.

He retreated into his kitchen area and I followed him aggressively into the brightness and carried on with my interrogation. 'The painting you sold me mush, where did it come from exactly?'

By this point Stevey had decided not to question my motives any further as he recognisably feared a serious slap.

'It's from a new artist in town. I only met him last week, but he comes highly recommended by Lord Terrance Trivago no less, and as such, has impeccable credentials I can assure you. There is no need to get upset, I thought you liked the picture having paid such a tidy sum for it?'

Stevey's sales technique was superb, only I wasn't buying this time. Instead, seizing him by his pyjama lapels like a latter-day Eric Morecambe and knocking his glasses off into the bargain, I began to spell out my demands.

'You're a director of the Tate I believe, so grab your keys, we're going to hang a new piece!'

Sitting at his kitchen table smoking, while I waited for the previously mirthful now frightened Mr Stevens to dress himself, I summarised the position fully to myself. The vampire-cum-recently-dubiously-qualified-artist, surely intended to attack this next night. With the painting hanging in my hallway, I had inadvertently invited his visit and, using the painting as his portal, he could cross over when he was ready, as soon as he saw me undefended and blissfully unaware within my seaside home. It was a nice plan, one that had a good chance of success, but I had decided to have a change of venue and shouted up the narrow stairs towards my new, furiously fumbling, subordinate.

'You're right Stevey, the painting is super-duper, so much so I think it is too good for my gaff and I am going to donate it to your gallery. When you're dressed I will be outside mate. No hurry, make sure you tuck your shirt in, got to keep up appearances.'

I lit up again as I waited outside the cottage, grateful for the thinking time. There was now a chink of light on the horizon, and I noted exactly where the sun was rising, as east, in this case, is always best!

By the time dawn had arrived, giving me the confidence that my undead would-be assassin had retired for the day into his own hidey-hole, my cooperative companion and I re-entered my studio apartment unseen due to His Lordship's negligent security, Flotsam and Jetsam, who no doubt lay in their own filth fast asleep still officially on the clock.

Taking care not to wake the delicate Booby and shushing Stevey, who was half in the doorway himself, I approached the painting and instantly pushed it face down onto the floor and re-wrapped it in its brown paper covering. With the picture secure under my arm we left the apartment as quietly as we had entered and made our way discreetly along the back roads into the deserted admission area of the Tate Gallery.

Stevey opened the door and neutralised the alarm system and now, more fascinated than frightened, beckoned me inward with my burden. The visitor reception area was stunning and exactly as I had imagined, plus, luckily, north-easterly facing. The huge Patrick Heron coloured window was resplendent in its glory and directly opposite I had Stevey remove the art piece that was currently hanging and replace it with the still enshrouded painting I had carried in with me.

'No need to unwrap it son, we will have a grand presentation soon enough and the covering will add the necessary intrigue and mystery.'

The hottest star in the morning heavens was now high enough to flood the area with warm sunlight and, checking the time, I saw it was near enough 5am and the mall area was spectacularly and colourfully bright.

Stevey looked to me for further instruction and I wasn't shy in giving it. I was also sure, thanks to a little autosuggestion, he was now to be trusted.

'Right keep your gob shut and everything will be hunky dory. When you open up this morning make sure you leave the wrapping on the painting, everyone will think that's the way it's meant to be in this place anyway! Make up a card to announce its arrival and make the dedication, 'From Maggie's T's as a gift to the gallery. In lieu of good taste, not taxes!'

It was clear he would do as instructed so we both departed, him back to his cottage and I on further, back to the studio apartment for a kip as if I had never even left.

'Oh, and by the way Stevey, let Lord Terrance know I have donated will you please.'

Before crashing out and without waking the slumbering Mr Booby de Faux, I took a picture on my phone of the view that the painting portal would have observed from its previous resting place across the hallway. Exhausted, yet satisfied, after such a workmanlike period of activity, sleep came blissfully for once and without a struggle, just as the early morning dog walkers and beachcombers did the best they could, considering the current restrictions upon their freedom.

St Ives shopkeepers in general are not known for being up with the lark and as I walked out of St EIA's small graveyard later that morning with a cardboard box that had previously contained a large pair of women's thigh boots according to the dirt encrusted legend on its side, I was amused to see quite a few potentials but disgruntled customers milling around. My old man was always out early on holiday looking for a café to have an early morning cuppa, but he would have been disappointed down this neck of the woods as it seemed 'Start late- Finish early' was the indigenous merchants' mantra.

Dead cats aren't heavy and not normally of much use either, but I had plans for what was left of the recently deceased Black Manilishi. Over and again, I returned, as I walked, to my worrisome problems and thoughts of the coming evening's probable events. If I hadn't taken the countermeasures necessary, De Havilland would have jumped out of the painting portal into the studio thanks to my unconscious annulment of the invitation clause. Then I assumed that not needing to attempt to drink my blood due to his recent top up and also as he couldn't have brought any weapons through with him, he would have undoubtedly either tried to strangle me or beat me to death with his bare hands. I shuddered as I considered a combination of the two would probably be his preferred option, for his own amusement if nothing else.

I was pleased to see in passing that Richard Soul had at least opened on time and as I entered his studio still carrying my cat coffin, I re-introduced myself with a request.

'Morning Dick, I need you to enhance a little picture for me, tout de suite.'

Looking up instantly and with a cheery response as if he couldn't do enough for his friends and customers these days, he ejaculated, 'No problem, Mr Crowley. What would you like?'

His offer was accepted, and I showed him the photo I had taken earlier within the apartment.

'Oh, just a little Photoshop manipulation. I've become very fond of my beachside lodgings and would like a replica. You're going to need a fucking big canvas the size of a wall because I need it in exact proportion.' It was a big enough ask as it was, yet he didn't even complain when, as I left, I threw a parting comment over my shoulder, 'I need it by tonight mate, I will have a couple of friends come and pick it up at about 10.30pm. Jump in the back of their van and come along as well, I am going to need all the helpful hands I can get tonight.'

At about the same time as I was making my way from Richard to see Phillip Browne at his swanky emporium, a phone call was ongoing between Lord Terrance Trivago and his reluctantly complicit sister Maggie as she struggled to serve both her waiting customers whilst holding back her tears.

'I'm sorry Terrance, how was I to know he would take the painting to the Tate?'

The pause in the conversation didn't last long as her irate brother raged back, 'You always were a self-defeatist useless waster, you silly little bitch! I won't forget this. You had better start packing, I want you out of my property today!'

And with that he replaced the handset as if he was swatting a fly while the sheepish Flotsam and Jetsam looked on, waiting for him to turn his ire on them, which he did without delay. 'So! You watched him all night, did you? You lying bastards!'

To add insult to injury, I am sure he realised there was no way he could stop any unplanned events taking place, his joint plan with De Havilland now shot to bits because he had no way to contact and warn the vampire, not of course being privy to the bloodsucker's whereabouts. The most he could do from this point on was hope for the best.

His best and my best were of course diametrically opposed and while he no doubt began to panic, I entered 'The Glory Hole', this time as a welcome guest, as Phillip looked up from behind his till and, without formality, offered his hand and best wishes.

'Hello Mr Crowley. Great to see you again. What have you got in the box?'

'Just a dead cat pal.' My answer was deadpan, and he thought, understandably that I was joking with him as he chuckled and laughingly replied, 'Hah, hah, well I'm glad I didn't sell it to you!'

I leant in toward him and continued, 'Need a favour Phill my boy. I require a large blind knocking up and I reckon you're the bloke who has the know-how and the skills.'

He raised his eyebrows. 'Well, you're right! That's up my street for sure. How big and what colour do you want?'

This new version of the previously snooty obnoxious retailer was a vast improvement and no request seemed too much trouble, 'Just blackout quality and seven by seven should do.' I replied.

He wasn't fazed, 'Oh, seven foot by seven foot is no problem. I will have that done in a jiffy for you.'

He did look rather flabbergasted with my next response and the subsequent instructions, however.

'No mate, seven metres by seven metres and I need you to bring it to the rear entrance of the Tate at 11pm tonight, no excuses. I'll have a few friendly geezers come and help you do the lifting and shifting.'

Again, I left another friend scratching his head and with my directives ringing in his ears,

'Cheerio for now Phill, don't let me down mate.'

With the cunning bits now arranged, it was time to rally more troops and secure the extra manpower needed. A phone call to Chopper from Booby secured the muscle, and a cuppa with Derek and Joan at the Coast Watch Station was not only a welcome interlude, but also productive when it came to acquiring some more of the administrative help I would need.

Anybody watching as I wandered into the Norse Stores and gained the commitment of Mandy and her new musclebound but badly bruised and nervous boyfriend, would have thought I had turned over a new leaf. My advances were this time accepted as genuine and although I didn't explain precisely what was to happen that night, they were both more than happy to help with the moving and grooving, as excitement in the town had been in short supply until my recent appearance and therefore was gladly welcomed by the younger members of its society.

My final call of the morning was to Maggie T's café. It seemed that I was just in time and as the church bell of St EIA's struck midday, Maggie was turning her key in the front door and standing with two forlorn suitcases at her feet. My surveillance had gone unnoticed, she looked distraught, and her panda eyes were as prominent as the 'Closed for Business' sign that hung inside the door. She gazed through into the darkened café for one last time.

'Going somewhere darlin'?'

Shocked, she turned, 'I… I'm sorry, I have made a right old mess of things Alex.'

I moved towards her and plucked the suitcases from the pavement, 'Don't sweat it doll. Some say pot-ate-o some say pot-at-o or in your case, some say Taylor but I knew it was Trivago!'

Her eyes fell to the floor and shamefaced she asked, 'How did you know?'

I didn't wait for her to follow so as I walked away with her cases I answered.

'You can't con a conman luv. Come on, you can still help to put this right.'

By tea-time my sap had risen fully, and I was ready to face my final summertime showdown. Booby fussed around the table back at the studio apartment while we tried to enjoy the salad he had prepared. I was hoping it wasn't going to be my last supper.

'Flipping wasps! If I get stung I will swell up like a balloon!' he complained.

Handing the phone to Maggie, I made my Judas request of her.

'Give that arse of a brother of yours a bell will you. Tell him to meet me at 4.30am tomorrow morning at the front of the Tate. Oh! And tell him he can bring his two monkeys if he wants protection.'

With that I returned to the St Ives Times and Echo. This week's headlines proclaimed, 'Long hot summer to continue as the Tate tries to attract the crowds to offset beach closures'. At least that jewel in the crown hadn't been affected. Yet!

The light was beginning to fade by 9pm and checking the paper again, I saw that the dawn was scheduled for 4.41am and the weather was set fine with another scorcher predicted. Happy days.

My next call was to Stevey Stevens. 'All quiet on the western front Stevey?' I inquired.

'All's quiet here Mr Crowley,' came the welcome response. 'Bring your people to the rear entrance at 11pm as arranged. I have given the cleaners the night off just as you insisted so we won't be disturbed, and you can be assured the painting is still wrapped and in place on the wall where you left it.'

Bang on the dot Stevey unlocked the huge rear entrance doors which allowed entry to any colossal sculptures and their like, ready for display. With Booby alongside, we pushed the doors open.

'Come on boys, time is tight,' was my brief jolly up.

Within ten minutes the Tate reception area looked like a posh building site. Chopper and his crew along with Phillip entered transporting a long roll of black fabric like a scaffold pole and they were followed in on cue by Mandy and her boyfriend carrying ladders. Next came Richard assisted by Maggie and the cycle sluts, Pearl and Suzy resplendent in their normal party wear of fishnets and leather jackets. The heels, they wore didn't suit the effort needed, but the three of them managed to transport the large picture-perfect canvas that Richard had created to its new resting place opposite Patrick Heron's coloured window all accompanied by some rather fruity language.

Booby had deigned to carry in the dirt-laden cardboard box containing the Black Manilishi's corpse at least and then Derek and Joan shuffled in, he with red toolbox complete with a hammer handle sticking out the side to emphasise his intent and she with a fully loaded tea trolley in tow, God bless her! I proudly looked on and with a lump in my throat gave the call to action, 'OK boys and girls. Let's get ready to rumble!'

Timing was key, so at 1.30am with the work well underway and all hands-on deck I made the call I had been dreading but always knew would have to come one day, 'I know it's late Reuben. I said I would call on you again my son and I wouldn't ask if it wasn't important.' I didn't give my taxi driving friend time to react, not that he could have anyway, as the suggestion spell I had supplanted in him upon my arrival in town weeks before kicked in, like a tramadol on the rocks. 'Yes, I know it's three hundred miles mate, but leave now and you will be here for a late breakfast. Thanks mate, you're a star.' It wasn't a request I knew he could repel thanks to my previous suggestive implant, so I was certain he would slip something suitable on and, like a trained zombie, be out the door and on his way before his missus could chew his ear off.

I gambled that De Havilland, the bloodsucking son-of-a-bitch, must be getting understandably a little impatient and frustrated, as he would have been awake for hours staring at the back of the brown paper wrapper that surrounded his portal. I was also pretty sure that he wouldn't dare an entry until he had a clear view of the scene that awaited him and only then if things looked kosher. Fucking risk-averse abstract artist vampires! What was the world coming to?

As I imagined he was indeed looking sideways on at an identical painting hung on the inner wall of the abandoned building on the headland that he had requisitioned as his base of operations. Alongside, his three feline wives watched him as he paced the dirt floor with murder in his heart, determined to strike as soon as he could. I knew the waiting would not help him to think logically and patience is happily not a vampiric virtue.

At 4am my band of merry men and women had completed their endeavours and I was more than thankful and bursting with pride. After thanking them à la Henry the Fifth, I made it clear that the battle was mine and mine alone from this point on, so my wonderful collaborators, excepting the ever loyal and necessary Booby, left us, reluctantly taking all their trappings and tools away along with my best wishes.

The canvas picture with the studio apartment view was standing at attention opposite the still wrapped painting and the vision upon it was a perfect life-sized facsimile of the apartment scene. The huge Patrick Heron coloured widow was draped with one of the biggest blackout curtains imaginable and the quick release cord hung untested down one side, strategically positioned near the one dimmer switch that Booby was poised to operate and darken the room suitably when I instructed.

Fashionably but predictably five minutes late at 4.35am, Lord Terrance entered through the front reception door, followed dutifully by Flotsam and Jetsam armed with baseball bats. 'The door was open Crowley so we let ourselves in.'

'Well done son. Early bird catches the worm or so they say,' resonated my sarcastic retort.

As this ghastly threesome stood on guard, cautious and suspicious no doubt of my relaxed approach, behind them unseen, arrived IA in full battle dress with Peter Green holding a collar and lead at his side. As always my own protecting angel had arrived in the nick of time and looked ready to do combat, although I knew this time, the real conflict could only be mine.

Keeping the aristocrat and his scruffy minders under my stare and at a typical duelling distance, I motioned flamboyantly and issued my directives, 'Would you like to remove the painting's wrapping Your Lordshit? I am sure you will enjoy the exercise. Oh! And Booby, dim the lights a little more if you please,' and before either could do as directed, I moved in front of the canvas and took my place as a willing, but nevertheless apprehensive, target.

The temperature in the room seemed to drop noticeably and in the concrete temporary den structure up on the headland the rustle of the covering paper was noted by De Havilland as he turned and peered deeply into his side of the dimensional gateway. The mock view he saw when the canvas was exposed was convincing enough and, with the light reduced to near darkness, he forgot any cautiousness. Predictably, he didn't check his pocket watch as he flung his body through the portal expecting to land in the studio apartment that was on deceptive display.

Landing a little inelegantly in his excitement, he assumed a crouched attacking pose. Then, realising he was not where he thought he'd be, he held himself in reserve, scanning the area. He also did no more than note Lord Terrance and his bodyguard's presence, along with that of Booby against the wall, who was now also clutching the oversized cardboard box under his right arm, while his left one was poised beside the dangling cord.

'What is this place Crowley? Another of your tricks?' questioned the frantic vampire.

'More an illusion my old cocker,' I countered, and that was enough to prompt Lord Terrance to make his presence fully known as he shouted toward our little mêlée, and in particular De Havilland, 'Kill him you fool! Strike now before he can flee!'

It was an invitation the vampire didn't intend to miss and in an instant he was on me knocking me to the floor of the gallery and with his hands clamped tightly around my throat.

'That's it!' encouraged the thrilled lord, 'choke the life out of the cocky bastard!'

With just about my last gasp, I gave my desperate order, 'Ur… urgh, now Boobs!'

Booby yanked on the sash at his side and, after a slight quiver, the blind fell like an oversized heavy petal and bounced hard to the floor. At this point De Havilland had released his grip on my throat with one hand and was enjoying the pummelling he was dishing out to my previously good looking boat.

I think I smelt the burning pork pong long before I saw any smoke. The dawn light raced in through the painted window now uncovered and fell like a magnifying glass's concentrated beam colourfully and squarely in the middle of the vampire's back. The pain must have been intense, and his grip faltered, then his awareness was replaced by panic and as I shuffled away on my elbows, I caught sight of a smiling IA, who I like to think stood ready to join in on my side, although I couldn't be sure. Then I heard the vampire scream, 'You burn me yet again magician… Arrrghhhhhhhhhhhhh!'

De Havilland staggered forward into the collapsed blind seeking shelter from the sun's colourfully abstracted rays, but no sooner had he obtained a modicum of cover, he burst into flames. The blind along with the canvas caught alight instantly and the bonfire raged instantly out of control.

Managing to gather my senses, I pulled the cardboard box containing the departed Black Manilishi out from under the stunned Booby's arm. Turning toward Lord Terrance who had not moved far, I stated in my throttled voice and holding the box outward, 'I owe this little guy my life. Now it's my turn to repay the debt properly. 'Ere, catch this, you pompous bastard!'

With that I launched the box in Lord Trivago's direction. All that public school boy rugby training hadn't been wasted and he instinctively caught it, like a South African Fullback, after it had looped high, pulling him inwards as if magnetically towards the fire as he made his frantic grasp. IA stepped forward and aiming her sword at the spectacle, there was a familiar blinding flash of yellow hellfire and the aristocrat fell headfirst into the flames along with his catch, already thankfully unconscious. The inferno was by now all engulfing and with the flames licking around our backs I gave sound advice to my traumatised friend, 'Come on Boobs, let's leg it!' He wasn't the only one to take my advice, as Flotsam and Jetsam managed to keep up with us as we fled, looking every bit like they were trying to get in our slipstream.

A crowd had begun to form outside opposite the Tate's rotunda and as soon as I felt we were suitably distant, I turned to see a sight I will never forget. The serene Peter Green walked away from the flames and down the road untouched, and more significantly, he had a young, strong, handsome and invigorated Black Manilishi on a lead at his feet.

By 11am the Tate had been reduced to a smoking husk. As a multitude of firemen dampened down the rubble, I sat alongside Maggie and Booby on the hard grey granite sea wall as we watched with pleasure as the local plod frog-marched the handcuffed Flotsam and Jetsam towards a police van. I didn't have far to look for a light for my cigarette but it was hardly in celebration as I spoke out, 'Never did go much for contemporary art, although I didn't mean to burn the bleeding place down!'

Booby chipped in loyally, 'At least you're still here and that's all that really matters Ally.'

A black London cab replaced the departing police van and I saw the familiar face of Reuben, spellbound behind the steering wheel. Maggie looked devastated as I turned and spoke kindly, 'Lady T tells me you will inherit half the Trivago fortune. Try not to be as big an arse as your brother hey?'

Then I turned to Booby. 'The studio apartment is signed over to you Boobs, along with a handsome monthly income via the late Lucky Lucian's estate. Sorry mate, I forgot to tell you, he croaked it last month. No great loss, mind.'

Placing a large brown envelope in my friend's hand, I concluded my bulletin.

'The rest of my holiday money is in here mate. I want you to divvy it up between Peter, Richard, Phillip, Mandy, Chopper and Derek and Joan. I am sure they will use it for better purposes than I ever could.'

Without further ado, I clamped his head in my hands and kissed him fully on his lips, much to his astonishment. Then more conventionally I did the same to Maggie as the tears streamed down her face. Quickly I stepped into the cab and as we accelerated away up the hill at the side of Barnoon Cemetery, I caught my final glimpse of the pair holding hands and sobbing.

At the top of the hill standing at the junction which indicated the farewell route from the town, stood the tiny figure with the large backpack. She raised her hand in salute and although I smiled and waved back, I must admit I choked my own tears down as we sped away. The view through the cab's back window was the opposite of when I had arrived. The welcome sign had a large red cross through it and the word 'Closed' as if daubed in blood. The glint of barbed wire twinkled from the beaches and smoke was still billowing from the site of the Tate.

Sitting back exhausted, I spoke my last words for the next three hundred miles, 'Take me home Reubs, I could do with a bloody good holiday!' As I drifted off to sleep, I'm sure I heard a distant, faint, 'Meoooooooooow!'

End

Author Bio

Don Barr? Author, artist, landlocked surfer, army brat, only child and lover (Of his dog at least!) A punk rocker attitude and a hater of the pompous and all airs and graces. Born in 1960. Not dead yet.

Connect with Don:

Email: donbarr@talktalk.net

Twitter: @onbarr

Facebook: https://www.facebook.com/don.barr.923